Black's Gold

by

Lori Power

McGuire Series, Book 1

Black's Gold

Cover Art by *Debbie Taylor*

The Wild Rose Press, Inc.
PO Box 708
Adams Basin, NY 14410-0708
Visit us at www.thewildrosepress.com

Publishing History
First Edition, 2021
Trade Paperback ISBN 978-1-5092-3552-0
Digital ISBN 978-1-5092-3553-7

McGuire Series, Book 1
Published in the United States of America

Flora crouched and edged her way closer to the pair. Recent rain made the stone wall slick and the ground underfoot perilous. He cleared his throat and she froze, so close now the pungent tang of ale and onions filled the space between them.

He laid a land over Maggs' traveling fingers. "You're not supposed to be here," he rasped and began to step away. The dim light exposed the gap in his teeth and a smashed nose. "I'm to keep the alley clear for the boss."

Maggs lifted a seductive knee to block his path. The movement caused the skirt of her dress to hike up her leg, exposing her thigh.

Flora waited for her moment. Waited for the signal from Maggs now that his attention riveted on her mother as the slippered foot slid down over his leg to his shin.

He swayed, shoulders swiveled, but still he didn't fulfill that first step.

Everything was in motion now. Maggs' fingers fluttered across the barrel chest, her lips nibbled the scruff of unshaven jawline, and her leg rose again so the garter holding her stocking showed just above her knee. Then she wrapped the sensuous limb around his waist.

Despite the aches Maggs often complained to Flora about, her mother moved like a faerie wood nymph. Graceful to the last. Clothing never mattered to any of their marks. Had they bothered to look closer, they'd have seen tattered clothing on an old woman. But in the moment, she sprang new again, fresh and available.

Praise for Lori Power

"A delightful, light-hearted romance that will assuredly fill the reader with only good thoughts."

~Lisa McCombs

~*~

"It's an interesting story and it's really unique at the same time."

~Samantha Dewitt

~*~

"A marvelous blend of mixed messages and tangled identities as two star-crossed lovers fall in love despite their families' histories of cut-throat competition in the banking world...This beautifully written story is filled with strains of soft jazz singing mingling with luscious images of warm Southern California evenings on the beach."

~Jack Magnus

~*~

"It is an awesome story. Beautifully written, with very credible characters. Loved the story and the outcome. Highly recommended reading."

~Patricia Day

Dedication

To the one who started it all, Mackenzie...at last

Chapter One

1767

From the other end of the dank alley, Flora watched as Maggs' hand slid across the man's ample shoulders. Her pulse kicked up a notch at the thought of the anticipated heavy purse. She and her mother had marked him out earlier as a money man. Surely, the day's gambling take would be just the score they'd been working for all these years.

As Flora kept watch from her hiding place, Maggs' practiced fingertips raked a seductive trail. The pale sheen of her bared skin practically glowed in the gloom and shadows. Then she pressed her generous breasts, corseted for maximum exposure, despite the chill, to his back and traced a line of intent down his torso to the fastening of his breeks. Maggs knew her trade well. Allowing his anticipation to build, she paused, palm hovering.

The man, taller by head and shoulders than Maggs, was no match for this performance. In fact, Flora hadn't seen a man yet able to resist. The brute, whom they knew to be part of Tommy Two-Guns' gang, inhaled sharply and stood still, putty in her mother's experienced hands.

Flora had seen the performance so many times she needn't watch. At this moment Maggs would rise up on tiptoes to flick her tongue so it connected with the lobe of his ear. Like most men this time of year, he wore a woolen cap against the constant batter of ocean weather.

Her heart slowed as she stretched her fingers and tightened her leg muscles. Her part in the recital came next. Maggs would ensure he was well distracted so Flora could do her job.

Flora crouched and edged her way closer to the pair. Recent rain made the stone wall slick and the ground underfoot perilous. He cleared his throat and she froze, so close now the pungent tang of ale and onions filled the space between them.

He laid a land over Maggs' traveling fingers. "You're not supposed to be here," he rasped and began to step away. The dim light exposed the gap in his teeth and a smashed nose. "I'm to keep the alley clear for the boss."

Maggs lifted a seductive knee to block his path. The movement caused the skirt of her dress to hike up her leg, exposing her thigh.

Flora waited for her moment. Waited for the signal from Maggs now that his attention riveted on her mother as the slippered foot slid down over his leg to his shin.

He swayed, shoulders swiveled, but still he didn't fulfill that first step.

Everything was in motion now. Maggs' fingers fluttered across the barrel chest, her lips nibbled the scruff of unshaven jawline, and her leg rose again so the garter holding her stocking showed just above her knee. Then she wrapped the sensuous limb around his waist.

Despite the aches Maggs often complained to Flora about, her mother moved like a faerie wood nymph. Graceful to the last. Clothing never mattered to any of their marks. Had they bothered to look closer, they'd have seen tattered clothing on an old woman. But in the moment, she sprang new again, fresh and available.

Flora often thought the attraction came from the draw of her mother's fiery red hair. She wore it loosely bound at her crown, which allowed it to fall in waves across the creamy skin of her breast.

"Always give them the promise of more," she would say to Flora while preparing for their evening work.

Flora had inherited the fiery red locks, though no one would know. In her mother's fiercely protective way, Maggs insisted Flora crop her hair and wear a cap to maintain the illusion of being a boy. In addition to the costume, she also added soot to darken both her clothing and her face.

Though she would never say as much to Maggs, she envied her mother's lustrous hair, the natural shine despite their squalor. At eighteen, Flora knew she couldn't maintain the guise for much longer. Even now her body was bound by so much strapping it cut her breath and impeded her ability to move as quickly as she once could. In their work, she needed to be fleet of foot.

Her mother considered the lack of swift mobility a small price. Flora knew better. In their profession, getting caught was only a matter of time. They were running against the clock and hoarded every brass penny to stay ahead and hopefully be gone before their time ran out. But that was a concern for another time.

Throwing the worry from her mind, she lifted a tentative hand to scratch an itch. Her nerves twittered as with electric current in anticipation of her role. She positioned herself close to their feet, in his blind spot toward his back.

"Come now, me darlin'," Maggs cooed, finally speaking in her husky tones. "We'll be fast about our business. Penny for a pinch, nickel for a tickle."

When he shook his head but made no move to part, Maggs oscillated and slid the cuff of her hand across the protrusion in his pants.

From her position, Flora saw the weapon hanging from his belt.

Maggs smiled up at him. "Oh, yes, not long at all."

With more vigor, a cough, and bending slightly away from her knowing touch, the man made to turn back to the alley entrance.

Quick as lightning, Flora watched Maggs pull the knife from its sheath at the man's hip. She held the blade just under his squared jaw. "Now, boy," her mother commanded. "Grab the purse."

While Flora sprang from the shadow, the man reared. His elbow caught Flora in the ribs and air gushed, but her mother, much stronger and certainly more agile than she looked, held firm and pressed the knife's point against the artery. She'd been a nurse in times better than these and knew the body more intimately than most.

"Now, now, me darlin'," Maggs cooed again in her husky tone. "I told you we'd be fast."

"Dirty bitch," he hissed through gritted, gapped teeth. His body angled to accommodate her shorter stature. "They'll get you for this. Do you have any idea who I am?"

Her mother tut-tutted. "No. But we can hope the papers get 'er right when you bleed out from the slice I'll leave in your throat if you do no' shut your hole."

Like a shadow, Flora snatched the purse attached to the man's belt. "Nah," she growled, assuming a masculine gutter drawl she'd perfected these last years to match her disguise. "You say a word and you'll be nothin' more than fish bait. Unrecognizable."

Flora gazed up into the man's face more than a foot above her. His lack of fear fueled her anger at their circumstances. The never-ending struggle for survival on these dirty streets. Her mother's dream of escape seemed as far away now as it had ever been. There was always one more mark, and still they starved.

She weighed the disappointing take in one hand, then tossed it to Maggs, who stashed it quickly away in the deep pocket of her ragged frock.

Taking advantage of Maggs' momentary distraction, all of a sudden the man bucked in Magg's grip. Her mother lost her balance and stumbled back two, then three paces, landing hard. A racking cough preceded Flora jumping up, reacting on instinct to grab the burly man, more fat than muscle, by the shirtfront and smashing her knee into his balls.

Satisfied by the surprise and whoosh of air as the man fell to all fours in the gutter filth, Flora didn't hesitate. She kicked him again, missing his face, landing the blow to his shoulder. He glared at her and, enraged, she curled her fist and smashed him in his lantern jaw. Her hand connected with bone, and pain shot up her arm in painful pins and needles.

"Enough now," Maggs said in a gasping wheeze.

"Be done." Maggs grabbed Flora's hand and they stepped back into the shadows. Small rasping noises marked where he lay.

"That'll hold him for a bit," Maggs said, huffing and gulping breaths. She bent at the waist. "By the blood, he got me good."

When Flora hesitated, raising her leg to kick him again, Maggs straightened and pulled her along. "Never you mind about ol' Maggs. Come away now, me love."

Of a similar size and build, the pair ran, stumbling through the back alleys, their steps echoing over the cobbled stones and marking their progress. With no shouts of pursuit, Maggs bade Flora to stop, clutching her ribs, a whistling wheeze her only sound. Arms wrapped loosely around each other, they paused, pushing their backs against the rough brick, and listened. From a nearby doorway, the high heckle of a woman in the throes of passion calmed them. These were the sounds of their home, where they survived.

Maggs drew an old rag from her pocket and leaned into the coughing fit which claimed her again. Flora noted the dabbling of blood on the material and turned her head away to scan the surroundings.

Waiting for her mother to straighten up, Flora took her mother's face in her hands. "You all right?"

Maggs stashed the handkerchief away, then cupped Flora's cheek. "We'll be fine, me love," she said, a smile splitting her face, the crooked eye tooth seeming to catch the meager light. "Be proud we took one o' Tommy's boys down. He'll get more than a smack, he will, giving up his purse."

Flora nodded.

"Tommy Two-Guns, they call 'im," Maggs said

with a cackle, gasping for air. "Named for wearing a gun each hip. Now, there be a mark for us."

Her mother drew her into a fierce embrace before stepping back, eyes bright. "You'll see…someday soon we'll be back in a home of our own. Come along, now, let's see what bounty we managed."

Flora didn't see how they'd ever manage a home again. Her father and brother were dead, and her memory of a life with them had faded to a blur. Only the stories her mother recounted of their earlier life kept the memories from being obliterated altogether from any recollection.

Soggy with sweat, anger boiling through her veins, Flora followed her mother through the labyrinth of side streets and alleys. Despite the chill of the north wind funneling through the streets, the air seemed musky with a life which occurred only after dark, like the wolves who once upon a time would venture onto their farm in search of easy prey. Flora felt a kinship rather than a fear for the night predator.

Before long they reached the hovel they shared with various vermin.

Her mother smiled her crooked grin as she tinkled the contents of the small bag she held. "Won't be long now and we'll have enough to put you on one o' those fancy boats and get you a fine future," Maggs said and kicked aside a wharf rat. She tugged the strings of the purse to release what it held. She counted and recounted the coins, then huffed. "Shame. No paper. Coin and some sort of leather pouch. Who carries a purse within a purse? Dumb as a stump, the fellow. Nothin' inside. Wait." She rubbed a hand across her eyes, blinking hard. "Scribbles of some sort. Can't see it the now.

We'll check in the morning."

Flora busied herself releasing the ties around her breasts and swayed with the relief of rapid air flow. Still, she couldn't imagine leaving her mother. She had to quit this talk of Flora going away. What would happen if they were separated? "Ma, I told you, I do not—"

"I'll no' hear a word." Maggs stooped to drop the remaining coins from her hands into Flora's father's saddlebag, the one remaining item from their life before. She held up the decorated purse. "'Tis a good piece of leather, this," she said, holding up the spare sack. "May be good for something. We could sell it. You never know."

She stashed the leather in a side pocket of the satchel, then tucked the bag, weighted with their earnings, back beneath the floorboard. Pulling the rag rug to cover the spot, Maggs straightened, winced, and grabbed her side, her back creaking with the motion. A pained smile lifted her lips when she faced Flora, her round eyes bright.

The flickering streetlamp light that managed to seep into the room through the cracks in the boarded window threw her mother's face into planes and hollows. Without having to see the color, Flora knew the soft blue eyes would be as fierce as the icy gales coming over the harbor in winter and penetrate just as deep into her soul.

"Seems yur whole life you've been playing the part of the lad, and now you don't see the future yur da and I envisioned for you as a lady—"

"For my protection—"

"Shouldn't have to be like this," Maggs cut in, a

slight warble in her tones. "A whore's life is not your future. Help me, God, it's not."

"Don't say that, Ma." A hard lump of emotion grew in her throat, limiting Flora's ability to talk. But she couldn't let it go. Even when she passed the fancy homes of the well-bred, she could never envision herself in them. Couldn't imagine how to even act the part for entrance as a servant.

She shook her head, resigned where her mother couldn't be. "Thievin's no better, but we're gettin' by."

Maggs coughed without end, and a spittle of blood emerged. The rattle, so alarming in its intensity, caused Flora to drop the subject, not wanting to further upset her mother and aggravate the consuming illness.

When Maggs finally caught her breath, she drew Flora close to peer through the crack in the boards where they could see the ships at anchor. "Yur da and Samuel are watching over you and know there's a better life," she said, the smile revealing a missing tooth on the left side where she'd taken a blow from a mark. "I may have done things I'll not be discussing with yur da in the afterlife, and he'll not ask nor hold it against me. And I'll continue to do it 'cause I know you'll not live here much longer."

Tears glistened on her mother's pale cheek. "He tells me, you see."

"Tells you?"

"Yes, my darlin'," Maggs said. "Yur da, he whispers in my dreams at night, and I know it'll not be long."

Gooseflesh rose on Flora's arms. Her mother had never said such things before.

Maggs' wide, beautiful mouth, capable of pulling

any mark to her, spread in a grin. "'Tis time to get ye gone from this miserable place."

Chapter Two

Mackenzie McGuire stood at the helm of his four-mast, full-rigged ship, the *Navigator*, and squinted into the setting sun. He flexed his fingers and reached to absently stroke the top of the large, coal-colored St. John's water dog who sat stoically at his side. Duke, with his scruffy coat and scarred face, represented the extent of his family.

Man and dog seemed to understand one another, Mack mused as he ruffed the dog's lopped ear. Both stared into the distance, searching the horizon where shades of blue met the gloss of deeper green-grays, looking for the haze of dun and purple, weary of naval patrols.

The snap of sails signified their turn to the west-nor'west. Propelled in the increasing gale, white caps foamed against the bow. Tiller, the watchman, thirty feet up in the masthead, had spotted land an hour before. If the wind held, they'd make their rendezvous the next day.

"Keep us a-clear of that God-be-damned graveyard Sable Island," he said to Hemsley, the bandy-legged quartermaster. Before her death, his mother would tell him often of his sire, a naval officer, who went down off that God-cursed island. "I'm in no mood to face this storm on them rocks."

"Aye," Hemsley said in a heavy accent. "No one's

ever ready for the graveyard."

To their stern, storm clouds gave chase. If they pushed, they could weigh anchor by nightfall in a reasonably safe cove off New Scotland. Keeping well out to sea and dodging the British man-of-war ships, they had been pushing for Halifax Harbour for the last week. The heavy cargo of island rum promised a hefty purse worth the risk. Their ten-pounders had been primed and at the ready the closer they got, as a safeguard.

Mackenzie reached inside, to the breast pocket of his long oilskin, for the spyglass. Shaking the implement to its full length, he was rewarded with the sight of the faint purple shadow on the horizon. He released a long-restrained breath he hadn't realized he'd been holding.

If only his mother had lived long enough to see him captain his own ship. Like his father before him, he'd been placed by a parent on board his first ship at ten. Always stoic, she stroked his cheek and bade him to do as he was told. "Someday, my fine lad, you'll earn a commission and buy your ol' ma a house."

Years later, hardened into manhood through a life at sea, he'd returned only to find she had died in the workhouse, a poor woman. Determined never to see one of his own reduced to such a fate in the future, Mack sold his commission and joined a gaggle of mercenaries to earn his fortune at sea. Now he captained a captured ship he'd rechristened and ran his own crew. Little by little he'd been able to amass some legitimacy in trade with ambitions to operate a fleet one day.

As though in agreement, Duke barked.

"Aye, lad, land abounds, and our reward awaits."

He stowed the scope back within the safety of his oilskin and absently drummed his fingers against his leg, pacing out an old piano composition, one from his childhood spent next to his mother at her one true possession of any worth. Recognizing the song, the words now playing in his head, he stalled the movement and smiled at the memory. That was another life. The life she had planned for him of a commissioned officer, setting his sights far above his lot.

He snapped his fingers twice and the dog heeled. "I'll be in my cabin," Mackenzie said as he strode past Hemsley.

"Aye, aye, Capt'in."

Land always meant danger to those on board the *Navigator*. Patrols, conflict, and obstacles to their missions. The men would want shore leave. Their carousing and women brought their own risk. He needed to be free of the cargo before they made port.

Closing the door to his cabin, he shed the coat and tossed his cap to the bunk. Riffling the nonsense of curls away from his face, he retrieved the key from his breeks pocket. While Duke walked in circles before curling onto his rug, Mack bent to open his chest. Belongings, spare clothing, his mother's picture were on one side; the other was cluttered with maps and missives.

In the middle, hidden under his journal, lodged his prize possession. The scrap of leather, which on first glance, if one didn't know better, may have been tossed aside as a mangled purse. Yet on close examination, it was a map which had been expertly sliced in half. Now, at long last, this golden purse of Blackbeard was his map.

He ran a hand over the scruff of his chin, trying to imagine where it led. He blinked and shook his head, casting his gaze to the next item. Alongside the map, secured by a lock, lay his diary, and under this, the assembled letters procured over the last three years. These, more than any cargo, amassed his future. And for this he must make landfall.

He unfurled the incomplete map outlined on the inside of a rough-cut leather pouch on his desk. He traced a finger along the contours of the island. He knew the spot. Christ Jesus, you couldn't be at sea as long as he and not hear the stories and wonder, but it was the how he needed. The navigation of the deadly traps. What this map revealed only took him to the entrance; he needed the other. Again, he wondered at the scale, doing the numbers in his head, then jotting notes in his journal.

Whoever had the other half, if they had any inkling—of course they would know—would be equally eager to find this drawing. If this led to what he imagined, Blackbeard's fabled hoard, the map could prove a more dangerous possession than the treasure it promised.

But he had a name and location for someone who either knew where to find the other half of the leather purse or possessed it himself. A danger on many levels, complete with all the typical hindrances. Land meant patrols and sure conflict. Blackbeard had been no fool and Oak Island a trap the old pirate planned and executed to protect what this very map indicated lay so close.

He needed…a sharp pain gouged the side of his left

eye. Absently, he traced the weal of a long scar which bisected his brow and ran along the very edge of his eye, where it forked, then resumed to finish at his jaw line. He shook his head, knowing the pain a phantom. Both a reaction and a reminder of the peril of battle. He laid his palm flat, ignored the tremor, and resumed his study of the faded outline with its barely legible print. Regardless the danger, he needed the other piece.

Mack sighed, leaned back on his chair, and cupped either side of his head, then laced his fingers at the nape of his neck. His eyes roamed the wide-beamed ceiling of his cabin, seeking a solution to this impossible task. Hopeless certainly without the other half of the map. Once obtained, for he saw no other means, they'd need to be able to work unobserved and unencumbered. Then there would be the weather, ever the unpredictable element. Sure, he could try to take on the island without the complete drawing, but the risks weighed even heavier. Given the time constraints and possibility of detection, he needed to be accurate.

In the open sea, he could best and outrun just about any ship of the line—French, English, even Spanish. Terra firma changed the odds. He opened his notebook and reviewed the last entries. Now was the time, there could be no doubt. Others would have heard the same whispers. There were no secrets at sea. Word of such a windfall spread with the change of tide and crew.

The happenstance prize of the map taken from a Spanish galleon just two months previous finally removed all speculation of the authenticity of the rumors of the high sea treasure. Everyone suspected Eddy Teach, better known as Blackbeard, had taken the coordinates with him to Davy Jones' locker back in '24.

But Mack now knew the truth. That the Spaniard had been bound for Halifax for a rendezvous before the final destination of Oak Island was confirmed through the captain's logs, which lay next to the map.

One boot tapped the edge of his bunk as Mack leaned farther back in his chair. He pursed his lips and relaxed into the pose. Angling his head to the side, he stared at Duke, who had shifted with the slap of growing waves and the sway of the ship.

"We must make the acquaintance of this Thomas— Tommy Two-Guns—Thorn."

Duke opened one eye as though to acknowledge Mack's voice but seemed unwilling to provide more effort.

"We'll see how he earned that mantle, eh, boy?" Mackenzie set his feet to the planked floor and sat up. He patted his faithful friend, then the stack of letters, and continued the conversation with the dog. "Our good Captain Pedro Alvares has had many correspondences with the enterprising Mister Thorn," he said with a smile as Duke closed his eye. "As they have never met in person, we will simply keep the appointment."

Only his most trusted men knew of their true destination. The remainder of his crew would be told upon their arrival. For now, they need only be concerned with liquidating the on-board freight.

The dog's ears perked. Duke lifted his muzzle and sniffed.

"I smell it too, boy."

Sulfur, salt, and brine. The kettle mixing a fine brewed storm, dug from the murky depths of the ocean. "Our Poseidon's in a rare mood."

He stood to glance out the porthole. The azure of

earlier had been replaced by hues of gray. Clouds boiled in the near distance, dark shadowed and tipped with white. While on most days the sea gave him a sense of adventure, a welcomed wanderlust, as the ship creaked and tightened her holds in preparation, today she offered a challenge of survival. This area of the Atlantic took more ships to its salty depth than any other.

Deliberately, he secured the port and replaced his papers. Holding a palm to the dog, he uttered, "Stay," then left the cabin. A slippery deck was no place for his four-legged companion, no matter how seasoned.

The sea never gave much warning. Grabbing the rails to keep upright while the ship tossed, he mounted the stairs and assumed his position.

"Capt'in astern," the officer shouted, alerting the men to his presence.

The gusty wind whipped his black hair from the queue at his nape and tossed strands about his rugged face. Moisture collected on the beard he hadn't bothered to shave recently. He felt the weight and scrubbed his hand over his chin. He again considered the value of tarring his queue to avoid such distraction. Then a wave took the side of the ship and stole the balance of two deckhands not yet tied. He quickly scanned the deck and the rigging. All had been battened down.

He drew his collar up against the onslaught of the wind. "Lash to the mast," he ordered, his words carrying above the crush and blow of the gale.

The men obeyed, tying lines around their waists to prevent their being sucked overboard with the increasing foam and fury. Hemsley positioned the nose directly into the rising swells to thwart a capsize by a broadside rogue wave. Mack nodded approval.

Tiller whistled a warning, and Mackenzie pulled his spyglass. "Bloody hell," he uttered. He could see nothing through the squall.

"Ship o' the line, sir," yelled the scrawny young watchman. Tiller had the eyesight of a hawk and the instinct of a falcon despite having the origins of prison bait. Mackenzie had picked up the sixteen-year-old in the Carolinas three years ago. He earned his keep as a dependable seaman who gratefully performed as instructed.

Though he didn't doubt Tiller's report, Mack needed to see for himself. He traced the glass along the horizon. "Damnation." This was the third encounter with the bloody English patrols since veering north. "Those self-righteous, self-appointed ambassadors of the sea. One of these days we'll take their guts for garters."

"Too right," the stout and bearded John Mahone shouted. Then before Mackenzie could reply, he'd taken hold of the stair railing, lifted his feet off the plants, and slid, like retreating tide, to the lower deck.

"All hands on deck," Mackenzie shouted without lowering the spyglass. "About ship!"

Despite the toss, this order initiated the tack of the sails to the wind for increased speed. He would fight when pushed, but he'd much prefer to wait the bastards out, or better yet, outrun them. Being this close to his destination, he'd need cover until they either lost interest or found a better mark.

With a rush of blood pumping through his veins with the thrill of the chase, Mac strode to the quarterdeck to address the sailing master. "Burke, where do we lose these bleedin' bastards?"

The brawny islander lifted his tattooed brows, which only served to accentuate the width of his nose. "Seventeen sixty-five and still the English and French think they fight for control over a sea which don't belong to 'em."

"Neither you nor I will convince them of that." Though only a few feet apart from the man, Mackenzie shouted to be heard over the roar of the wind and the slap of the ocean. "Us paying a visit to Poseidon at the bottom of this bloody ocean won't alter the argument either way."

"Aye," Burke replied, more of a grunt as he leaned over his table of weather-resistant waxed charts, rain running off his bald head the color of polished oak. Never a man to hurry until he was sure, he finally answered when Mack slapped a palm to the side of the map. "On course, there are a series of small islands off New Scotland, what they now call Nova Scotia. We'll either be able to take cover there or lose them in between."

"You're familiar?"

"Aye, sir. I am that," Burke confirmed, standing to nod. "I was a pressed-to-duty man for years prior to joining your company, sir. We sailed in and out of these waters on patrol."

"Ah, yes, I recall." Mack blinked away the rain and stared into the gathering gloom before turning his attention back. Broad and stout with his wide, flattened nose, Burke wasn't a man to be reckoned with. He'd earned his place quickly since taking his post. When they took the Spaniard, Burke proved he could hold his own in any battle, making the younger hands wonder at the source of his facial scars.

"With some swift tacking, we could evade anyone following in there and make for Halifax just the same," Burke said as he bent, prepared to adjust the course.

Hemsley nodded agreement, standing within hearing distance, awaiting instruction. Then he took a firm hold of the wheel to steer them into the wind.

The sails cracked like gunfire and the ropes keened in protest. The planks moaned above the roar of the storm, and Mackenzie felt his ship buck the change. After a long pause where everything seemed to stand still, held like his breath, waiting for the change, finally, the lady that was his ship took the bit, and they all lurched at the new speed. Mack scratched the back of his head and paused but a moment to consider the map etched in his brain of the rugged eastern coastline before nodding approval.

"Good," he barked, his voice resonating above the melee. "We're in the lee of the wind, and if luck be with us, they'll not have noticed if we stay three miles over the horizon."

"Mayhaps they be in preparation for the storm," Burke said.

"Mayhaps," Hemsley agreed with a slight question, bespoke more from his sun-weathered features than in tone of voice. "Depends on whether they were in the storm when we a-spotted them or ahead of it as we were."

"Aye," Mackenzie agreed.

Feet spread against the whipping wind, Mackenzie faced into the storm without being lashed to the mainsail. An elation akin to the sensation of defying the elements—skimming above the confines of the ocean, ignited his nerve endings. His magnificent fifteen-ton ship with its twenty-pound guns moved as fleetly as a craft half its weight. Let this blasted Britisher try and catch us, his mind bellowed. He'd long ago separated his native country from those aboard the fleet.

They'd lost sight of the frigate, and night descended, almost unnoticed through the angry gray clouds, like the wings of a raven. Darkness swept across the raging, boiling mass until they were moving at speed without stars or moon to navigate, blind save their instinct and knowledge of the tides and currents.

They kept on, assuming the chase. Most of the crew had been pressed men of the Royal Navy, an experience that told them not to underestimate their enemy but assume pursuit. To maintain morale on what he knew would be a long night, Mackenzie ordered the boatswain to issue a tot of rum to all hands.

Steadfast to their course, soaked, sore, and hungry, they saw dawn finally bruise the horizon. Though the sea remained high, boiled to a fine rage, the wind had lessened. As the squall abated, a thick fog blanketed the rig. One hazard replaced the other, leaving them as blind as the night.

"Devil be damned," he murmured, hating to lose their advantage of speed. "Half mast."

Long fingers pinched his nose, and then he flung the dew of droplets from his lashes, and lifting his hat, he shook his head. Facing both the sailing and the quartermaster, he pointed to the charts. "Take us in."

"Aye, aye." They echoed in unison.

When it comes to acoustics, a socked-in fog mutes and amplifies sound at the same time. Moving through the mist meant they could well sail through the system and come out into morning sunshine. Who could say if their pursuers were not on the other side? All on board were aware that although they may not be able to see the British warship, it didn't mean they couldn't be heard, and to be heard would be to be found. No ship of war was above firing a shot, just in case.

"We will make the lee of Cornwallis Island by the end of the day," Burke said, no longer raising his voice above the weather.

Mackenzie nodded. He'd done all that was required at present. "See that we do," he said as he left the deck for the first time in hours.

The rendezvous placed them close to the docks and marketplace, provided they remained out of sight. The island took its name from Governor Cornwallis, who founded the city of Halifax after having lost control of the fortress of Louisburg fifteen years earlier.

Mackenzie retrieved Duke from his cabin, seeing him no worse for the storm. Together, they made a tour of his ship, greeting the men as they walked, the dog close and in stride at his side. He checked the rigging and ordered the boatswain to allow the men their rotation of much deserved rest and rations. Leaving Hemsley in command, Mackenzie too retired to his bunk.

****

Three hours later, dog at his side, the sun yet to show its face through the gloom, Mackenzie returned to the deck.

"We will be rounding the basin as the sun sets," Burke said, not waiting to be asked.

"What sun?"

"Too true, sir."

"Tiller," Mackenzie shouted.

"Here, Capt'in."

"What news?"

"No sign," the young man answered. Sopping clothing hung from his skinny frame.

"Have you not taken your rest today?" Mackenzie turned to raise his brows in question back on Hemsley. "Did I not order the rotation?"

"Scoot fell in the drink through the night and cracked his skull as we dragged him back," Tiller answered, speaking of his relief. Not many could scale the rigging like the monkey boys, as they were referred. "'Twas not safe for 'im just the now."

"He's lucky he remembered to lash," Hemsley said.

Mackenzie turned back to the boy. "As there's been no sign, take your rest. You're no good to us if you too fall from your post."

"Aye, sir."

"I've the helm, gentlemen." Mackenzie addressed both men. "You two are relieved. I'll hold the course and call you promptly at six bells."

"Aye."

"Good," Mackenzie answered as he paced the decks. Now calm, the sea seemed to heave with the effort of the storm behind them. Deep swells rolled at regular lengthy intervals. He ran a palm over his freshly shaven chin. Heated salt water was no substitute for a fresh bath, but they reserved the fresh for drinking and cooking. Before they landed, he would change his clothes, don the freshly polished boots and his cravat to look the part of the businessman.

He pulled his spyglass and scanned the horizon. Any business conducted depended on whether they lost their companion. Mackenzie knew not many a brig would maintain pursuit through storm and dark without making a move one way or another, but caution forbade assumption.

Six bells heralded a fresh crew, the night of high sea now behind them. "All hands hoay!" Mackenzie called and, without effort, his voice carried to every section of the ship. "We're for land, boys. You know what to do."

Mackenzie allowed a small smile to touch his full lips as he noted with satisfaction that there was no sign of any patrol. For now, and once again, he had escaped.

He turned to his sailing master. "Mister Burke, take us ashore."

Chapter Three

Flora eased from the spread of ragged quilts, careful not to wake her mother. It had been a long night, but finally, Maggs slept peacefully, no more rattle.

Fog puffed from Flora's lips with every breath. Grateful for the ease of her own breath, unbound from the bindings across her breasts, wrapped in a tattered shawl, she quietly knelt to start a meager fire from scrounged coal and debris. Though they garnered no paper money, the purse had been heavy with coin, and perhaps she could convince Maggs to splurge for some coal and a fresh loaf of bread.

Flora's stomach growled in anticipation. She splashed some water over her face and hands, dressed, and decided she would go to the market anyway. She'd surprise her mother with some real food not procured from trash heaps. Careful to the least amount of noise, she eased the board from under the strip of rag and pulled two coins free.

Casting a furtive glance toward her mother, biting her lip, she released her teeth from their task and smiled with the expectation of Maggs' wonder. How long had it been since Maggs woke able to appease the ever-present hunger of their existence?

In repose, Flora could see the beautiful woman her mother had once been. Though still striking and able to wield her body in a way too many men could never resist—the clink of coin proof enough—once Maggs had had a softness, an unvarnished warmth. Not the pointed edge of bones with scant enough meat to differentiate between alive and corpse.

Maggs had been a lady once. Well, a lady's maid, Maggs often corrected, but Flora knew 'twas the same. Flora loved to hear the stories of how her mother worked in a big house and enjoyed its three generous meals a day, beautiful clothing, roaring fires, and twinkling candlelight. So many waxed candles were held in storage they barely burned to half measure before being replaced. Oh, the extravagance! Her da had worked there as well; that's how the two had met.

Then the young heir, home from school, had taken notice of Maggs. How could he not? As Flora stared at her mother, she shook her head. Dirty and scruffy though she may be, no one with eyes could overlook the beauty of Maggs.

But where others may have not, her mother had resisted the young master, though he was insistent. Situated in a remote wing of the house away from others, no one heard her cries for help. Her da, who'd already won her mother's heart by that time, had gone looking for his lady love and took action, saving her virtue, Maggs would recount with a soft smile.

Flora swiped a tear, imagining the pair making a run for it, gathering their belongings and everything of value they could muster, and boarding the first ship available, bound anywhere. Bound for this new world.

"Ha," Flora hissed.

She rubbed a hand over her cropped hair. It was Flora's resemblance to Maggs which had provoked the costume to disguise her as a boy. "Your da always said you were my mirror image."

Mirror in image only, Maggs would say while running a gentle calloused finger across Flora's cheek. "But like your da in disposition, and more importantly, brains."

Then, if the moment were right, Maggs' crisp blue eyes would take on the faraway look when about to recount a memory of their life before.

"Oh, he had such a way with words and made me feel like a queen for a kingdom he would beat out of this new earth across the ocean and away from those who would see us as fit only for tenant farming," she would say. "If we were going to farm, let it be our own land. And someday, we'll get all that back for ye."

Flora blinked rapidly to stem the flow of emotion, noticing the spiderweb of lines scurrying from Maggs' closed lids. The lashes almost invisible, they were so light, highlighting the deep purple shadows beneath. The full lips, which had been punched to a pulp so many times they had lost their original rosebud shape. Flora wondered, at times like these, reflecting on the life they now lived, if her mother would have preferred to give in to her employer's advances. Would she have been any worse off?

She shook her head. Her mother would hear no such rebuke. Today, Flora determined, they could afford for her mother to be treated in some small measure like the lady she once had been, even if that only meant a breakfast they didn't have to scrounge from bins like stray dogs.

A woolen cap pulled low across her brow tended to conceal her identity as much as the baggy, dun-colored clothing and rough, sooty hair. She walked a brisk pace to the market where the morning aromas assaulted her senses to tantalize her hunger. Her mother's voice from the night before echoed and consumed her thoughts. Unfamiliar hope filled her. Today she wanted everything in sight: rolls, fish, a ham hock, sugar for their tea, and material for a dress. Flora had never worn a dress and wondered what it would feel like to have people look at her in her natural form.

A tingle on the nape of her neck preceded the rough shoulder which pushed her out of the way. "Watch where yer goin'," the grizzled voice snarled. Before moving off, he grabbed her face in one rough grip and then pushed her away. "Too skinny a lad for what we're after."

Flora stumbled, then sidestepped, fists ready, an equally abrupt retort poised on her tongue until she caught sight of the badge. Casting around, she noted three more at various locations. A prickle of fear coursed her spine. Something was afoot. She was only a block from the hovel she shared with Maggs, and her mother was alone.

Flora turned in the opposite direction, intent on a roundabout return to her mother when a hawker's impatient question stopped her. The uniformed officer barked at the top of his voice, ensuring all around could hear. "You know them or where they are, you'll do yourselves no good harboring them. Two wanted for murder."

Murder? Who? Flora watched the heavy man's progress through the market square.

"Two," another man yelled directly behind Flora and pulled her up by the scruff. "You know the whores around here?"

Flora shook her head, her cap coming askew. Grabbing it before it fell off, she uttered in her lowest tones. "Dem all whores 'round 'ere. Name yur price and I'll find ye just the piece yur after."

"Be off with ye, guttersnipe, before I take ye down the alley and teach ye some manners."

Flora lowered her head and began to take off, propelled by the swift boot to her backside the officer saw fit to place to cement his warning. As she rounded the bend, gasping to catch her breath more from fright of her mother being alone than fear for herself, she paused and peeked back.

"Nobody knows nothin' here, Harry," the man barked with a shake of his head. "We don't know 'twas a whore, and certainly Jimmy's only guessing two. No whore I know could 'ave bested a man as quick with a blade as Cain."

"So yur saying a phantom of what killed ol' Tommy Two-Guns' son," the companion replied, crossing the street in time with his mate Harry. "A ghost, I tell you."

****

Flora brushed her knuckles against her eyes, stilling the cold fear wedged deep in her gut. She would not cry. She would not panic. Maggs wouldn't want that. When finally she'd gotten around the swarm and back to Maggs, her mother was already dead.

She pushed her back against the rough stone wall of the alleyway outside the market. Lacing her fingers above her head, she slid down the wall into a crouch and pushed the cap down farther in an attempt to disappear. If she couldn't see, then maybe she wasn't really there.

A swift thwack to her thigh, followed by the pain to make her wonder if her leg had been removed, devolved this notion. "Outta 'ere," a man yelled, his apron covered in animal bits. A metallic tang of sweat, blood, and grime wafted with him. "I'll not have the likes of you scaring off customers."

Despite the agony, Flora wobbled to her feet and stumbled off as the man pulled his leg back for another strike. She faltered and fell but kept going. Still, she'd no idea where she could go.

Her hands shook when she pulled her jacket around her thin shoulders. She sniffed and tried to swallow the lump in her throat. Maggs was all she had, and she shouldn't have left this morning. Maybe it wouldn't have made a difference, her mother would still be dead, but at least Flora would have been there when the last rattled cough took her.

"Damn it," she uttered as a wave of grief threatened to swamp her with nauseous pain as acute as a knife wound. What would she do without her mother?

Moving without seeing, Flora relived the last hours, analyzing, questioning her every step. How could she have known, after the policeman stopped her and she raced back to the hovel to see Maggs lying as contentedly as when Flora left, that her mother was dead? "Come away, Ma," she'd cried, urgent in her tone. "Come away. The coppers are onto us."

She'd known. Sure, she'd known when Maggs didn't respond. Yet again and again Flora tried to shake her awake. But her shoulders were as cold as the frost that layered the rafters above in winter.

"No, Ma," she said, fighting a sob that she knew if

released would turn into a scream. "Come away now."

The pounding of feet on the landing below shocked Flora into action. "Oh, Ma…" She bent to kiss her mother's icy cheek, and just before she made to leave through the escape hatch in the roof, she remembered Da's satchel. The noise drawing closer, Flora's hands trembled to the point where she could barely skim the rag rug out of the way, let alone raise the splintered plank. Yet she managed somehow and replaced the board, too, flicking the material over the spot. She cast Maggs one last glance before hiking herself up and out of the trap door.

Now, as she lurched along blindly, the satchel seemed as conspicuous as if she were wearing a sign, inviting people to rob her. Where would she go now? She couldn't trust anyone. She had no one. Maggs had drilled that into her from their first day. "Nobody's a friend here," she'd said over and over again.

Flora sniffed, and the brine of sea filled her. Close to the waterfront but away from the bustle of the market, she traversed the length of the sea wall until she came to its natural end by the rock face of a cliff. Gasping for a breath, willing air to fill her starving lungs, she leaned against the slimy barrier, latching like just another barnacle. The ocean crashed, only feet away on the other side, the mist soaking through the shabby coat.

The grumble of approaching voices brought her to her feet. Searching the area, she considered returning the same way she had come or trying to climb the rock face. What if they were coppers and found her with the satchel? She'd be hung for the thief she was, let alone pinned to the murder of that man they called Cain.

Surely a boot to the ballocks hadn't kill a man. The rumbling tones drew closer to the bend in the wall. They'd be upon her soon if she didn't make a decision. She cast around, trying to decide, and threw her head back to gaze into the sky, seeking answers. There she spied a crack in the rocks above. She was tiny enough to fit, she knew. It was worth the try. If she didn't fit, she could hold still, hoping they wouldn't look up, or she'd have a head start and either make it to the top or let the sea claim her.

Luck she attributed to her mother's ghost gave her the strength to scrabble up the jagged rocks, and what had looked like a tiny crack opened into a sizable cave. She scooted through just as the men's voices turned from mumbled sounds lost to the wind into distinct words in which she could place meaning.

"No way that whore they called Maggs bested Cain."

Hearing these words, Flora positioned herself, belly down, head at the cave entrance. She shimmied forward to grab a glance.

She recognized the man from the morning, remembering he had been called Henry. While she watched, he lifted his cap to scrape stubbed fingers over the skin-damaged, scantily haired dome before replacing the hat. "That one was no bigger than a penny and Cain at least double her size."

"They found the knife Tommy Two-Guns had made special for the boy in her blankets," replied his wide-shouldered companion, hands lodged in his pockets.

"No' make sense. Her dead too." Henry's voice more nasal then the other.

They stopped where Flora had been moments before and turned to face the white-capped waves crashing against the boulders. Fog threatened on the horizon, rolling at leisure toward the shore.

"Umm." The burly man nodded.

When he made to turn back to face the path, Flora slithered back to tuck her head against the rock face.

"Froze to death, they think."

"No blood on the knife," Henry said. "Checked it myself."

"Doesn't change that there's the corpse of Cain, and Tommy'll be looking for blood hisself unless we pin it on the woman."

"But they said she was always with a lad," Henry said, turning to face back toward the muddied lane. "We present the boy to ol' Tommy and we're set for life. Leave it at that."

The tempo of Flora's heart hitched to a speed worthy of a horse on the run. The men had started to walk away, and she leaned out of the cave to grab what she could of the conversation before they disappeared.

"We've a decent description," Henry said, arms moving with his words. "You wanna catch a rat, you gotta scourge the gutters."

His companion's laugh carried them around the bend and out of hearing.

A sob escaped, and Flora covered her gaping mouth with her hands. "Bloody hell," she moaned. Every curse and blasphemed utterance she'd ever heard followed in succession.

She had to escape. Whoever killed this Cain would want her presented to Tommy Two-Guns as much as the two men she'd overheard.

Sniffing, she knuckled her eyes and swept at her running nose until both were dry. Maggs would stand for none of this blubbering. She peered at the filth of her cracked and dirty nails. Flea bites itched under the ragged clothing, and she scanned the garments, then removed her cap. She studied the brim, which had lost its structure long before Maggs pilfered it from an old man who may have been dead at the time. The disguise so long used for her protection was now the means of her destruction if she couldn't find another.

Rising to her knees, she pulled her father's satchel from where she'd hidden it beneath her clothing and, after scanning the outside of the cave, dumped the contents. It had begun to rain, and although she was protected from the brunt, the damp claimed her. It would be a cold night without another body to keep her warm.

She hiccupped and shook her head. Poor Maggs would never again be warm or able to offer any warmth. "Then let's not let your hard work go for naught," Flora said, more to buoy herself, hearing her mother's voice in her head.

With careful deliberation she counted the coins. Her mother had been sure they were close to being able to book passage—somewhere—anywhere. Flora prayed as she counted that Maggs had been right. Settling back on her haunches, she wondered how her mother would handle the situation. The coins slid through the gaps in her fingers, the soft tinkle as they landed providing some reassurance.

Standing, she paced the small area, hands on her hips. Feeling the natural curve of her waist and the sway her mother had started to comment upon, she

firmed to her resolution on how to get out.
"First a bath, then a clean frock."

Chapter Four

Light in the holds, the *Navigator* sat high in the water where she was moored, one of many, in Halifax harbor. Only a skeletal crew remained while the rest, randy and ready to part with new wealth for companionship, had taken their leave ashore.

Mackenzie shrugged into his coat and whistled for Duke to jump aboard the sloop. He yelled back to Hemsley, who stood at the stern, "I'll be back by six bells."

"Aye, sir."

Autumn colors of reds and golds decorated the coast as they rowed for shore. If he were so inclined, he could make a home in such a place. He scratched Duke between the ears. "Not yet, though, me lad," he said, staring at the throng of people along the wharf. "Not just yet."

Ensuring the golden purse was tucked safely away where the talented fingers of pickpockets wouldn't seek it, he jumped from the rowboat and onto the dock. "You're to stay here," he told the seaman, Tiller. "When I'm done and you bring Hemsley ashore, you may join him then."

A large snaggle-toothed grin provided enough assent for Mack to take his leave.

Mackenzie snapped his fingers once and Duke joined him, heeling at his side and matching his stride through the crowd. Coming to the edge of Water Street, Mack paused to gather his bearings. The banker, for the expected payday of the other half of the map, was how he had come to think of this Thorn. And what a payday it would be if he were able to keep Alvarez's arrangements to meet Thorn, secure the other half of the golden purse, and go after Black's gold.

He shook his head to clear his thoughts. Never count the coins until they're weighted in your own holds. He'd learned that a long time ago. According to the dispatches, Thomas Thorn did business on Barrington, two blocks north of Water.

Something shiny, like the reflection of the sun in a mirror, blinded Mack for a moment, causing him to halt and take in his surroundings. He paused mid step. A tingle raced along his spine and set him on high alert. He couldn't locate the beam. Duke too hesitated, either experiencing the same apprehension or picking up Mack's discomfort. Either way, the hackles along the dog's mighty neck rose.

Mackenzie held out a flattened palm to stem any growl, which would draw more attention. The dog pulled his ears back but obeyed. Mack reached under his coat, along his belt, to the flintlock tucked in its holster. He hovered his fingers along the wooden handle but refrained from drawing it out.

Thorn sounded like a vulture from the notes Alverez had jotted in the margins of the missives. But who wasn't these days? Dangerous or not, it was unlikely Thorn knew of Alvarez losing his ship. And if he did, more doubtful still that he would know to whom, and further that the same would be arriving in Halifax on this date to meet. Yet…

A well-connected man had eyes and ears everywhere. Could be he heard of the *Navigator* coming to port and meant to meet him here in public, take what he suspected was in Mack's possession, and be done with the whole affair. That is what Mack himself would do in the same situation.

After a sharp-eyed perusal of the area, Mack relaxed only slightly. He'd learned long ago to trust his instincts. Feigning a need to adjust his boot strap, Mackenzie bent, then scanned the area.

The source of his heightened sense became apparent when he spotted her. Now that he had her in his sights, his concern struck him as almost comical.

Also seeming to pretend indifference to the surrounding bustle stood the thief who had put him on alert. Unconcerned, he stood and tweaked his cap, his newly shaved cheeks raw against the bite of the wind without the accustomed protection of his beard. There could be no question she had marked him. Though she leaned lazily against a lamppost, a clearly laughable pose for a female of any age, her gaze trailed him under the brim of an overlarge bonnet.

It had been the man with the pocket watch at the other end of the pier whose reflection first blinded Mack. As he cast his glance between the two, he could discern no connection between the doxy and the lantern-jawed man. Though the man gave him no visible reason for concern, there was something about his shifty-eyed presence which had Mack take note.

As he stepped farther into the crowd, keeping a sidelong watch on the girl, he almost smiled at the tiny form and the slight threat she posed. He glanced back for another look at the glowering man with the pocket watch, as he'd learned a long time ago to trust his instincts, and something was afoot. The man was gone.

Perhaps she was not the source of the threat, or she could be a mere patsy for the man. Thorn? Certainly, the man didn't earn the moniker of "Tommy Two-Guns" through charity work. Either way, Mack had dawdled enough and needed to meet the banker. He would deal with whatever came his way now forewarned.

Taller by a head more than most, Mack covered the distance in good time. For a wee lass that he'd seen on the waterfront to keep pace, she'd need almost to run to keep up. The haste of such movement would certainly draw unwanted attention her way. He stopped to check the time. Tilting his head back to reaffirm the address on the front of the building, Mack also serendipitously scanned the street. Duke's ears remained alert, but his hackles had softened. No sign of the man or the woman. His shoulders relaxed only a fraction as he stooped to pat the large dog's head.

"You're a good fella."

Then he knocked.

A liveried manservant answered the door, his perceived authority far surpassing his height if the tilt of his nose and the line of his lips left Mackenzie in any doubt in judging his character. But the meaty fists held tight to his sides gave every indication of a man capable of holding the door when necessary.

Mackenzie did not alter his gaze. "Mister McGuire," he announced to the servant, removing the tricorn hat. "Standing in for Captain Pedro Alvares' appointment to see Mister Thomas Thorn."

The butler raked Mackenzie from stem to stern, as

the saying goes, and while he may not have found him lacking in any way, the domestic seemed reluctant to grant admission. When the man averted his pea-sized stare to the dog, his eyes widened at the sight and size of Duke. This provided Mack a trace of pleasure, for Duke's strong jaws, proven in many a battle, could snap this servant's neck in an instant.

While Mackenzie remained silent, the man's confidence diminished somewhat with each rapid blink. Silence, Mack knew, was a weapon seldom used, and for that reason Mack wielded it as efficiently as his saber.

Finally, the butler cleared his throat, stepped to the side, and swung his arm wide, indicating the hall beyond the threshold. "Right this way, sir."

"Thank you," Mackenzie said, crossing into a lavish entryway, Duke tight at his heel, sniffing the air.

"If you will follow me, I will show you to the sitting room." He turned his head in the direction of raised voices originating from a cavernous hallway opposite to their direction. "Master Thorn is presently in a meeting. I shall announce your arrival." Then he glanced down at Duke. "Will your dog be accompanying you?"

Mack nodded and stood fixed to the spot while the servant departed through the doors.

Left alone, Mackenzie strolled the parameter of the room, his steps muffled by the thick carpet. The walls featured many gilt-framed portraits, all shapes and sizes. Could someone possibly know or be related to so many? In Mack's opinion, this wrote the story of a man inventing generations of relations, relatives he perhaps wanted, more than those actually related by blood.

More show than class.

After a bit of a wait, determined steps approached the closed door. Mack turned at the sound.

Dressed regally in velvet and an overabundance of lace, the man Mackenzie assumed to be Thomas Thorn paused in the large doorway. Of average height, Thorn gave off an immediate air of a much larger man.

"Mister McGuire?"

"Mackenzie McGuire." Mackenzie stepped forward with his arm outstretched. "Mister Thomas Thorn, I presume."

Thorn shook the proffered hand. "Forgive me," he said, and Mack noted the dead-eyed stare of a shark in the regular features of the face. "I have recently lost my son and must have forgotten we had an appointment?"

Mack released the grip, stepped back, and tucked his thumbs into the waistband of his breeks. He nodded his head before raising his gaze to again meet the direct stare of Thorn. "My condolences."

Mack retreated into the middle of the room, allowing room for Thorn to enter. Letting the silence hang to add weight to his words, Mackenzie waited for Thorn to either continue a conversation or request him to leave.

Thorn moved to the decanter along the opposite wall, held up a glass with a raising of his bushy brows in question.

Mack nodded, then accepted the small measure of amber liquor.

Thorn sipped his own drink and lowered the glass back to the table. "A man with two last names," Thorn said with a smirk, the crooked teeth stained and chipped. The implied humor didn't reach the coal of his eyes. Thorn eased himself into a winged chair and waved a hand for Mack to follow suit.

Mack sat, then shrugged. "My mother had no brothers and I no siblings. I think she feared losing all lineage of the family name," he said, taking another sip of the fine spirit, waiting, on alert.

After another elongated silence, Mack gave up any effort of pretense. In light of the man's loss, Mack decided to come straight to the point. "I'm in possession of the correspondence you had with the former Captain Pedro Alvarez."

The hard eyes squinted, and the brows drew down to give his nose an arrow-like impression. "Former." Thorn stood and paced the room. He paused and stopped in the middle. His stance widened, square to his shoulders. "An acquaintance of yours?"

Mack gained his feet and set the crystal on a side table. Despite Mack's towering height, he didn't underestimate Thorn's compact frame. For the moment, he had no wish to make this man an enemy. At least not here and not yet. The recent death of the son, and he had no reason to doubt the black armband, put the meeting at a further disadvantage.

"Acquaintance…" Mack let the word hang. "Acquainted? Could be."

"As cryptic an answer as I've ever received." Thorn's gaze tracked Mack and then focused on the dog before he nodded, seeming to make a decision. He strode the length of the room to the cheery fireplace, its fire snapping and crackling in the grate. A golden cord hung to the side, and Thorn pulled it once.

Mack heard the tinkle of a bell in the distant bowels of the house.

In a moment, the door opened, and the butler stood, arms firm to his side.

"Refreshments for our guest, Donnelly," he commanded.

Once Donnelly left, Thorn turned his gaze to Mack. "Let's resume our seats, Mister McGuire—"

"Mack will suit."

With an ease Mackenzie felt sure was forced, Thorn flopped into a wing chair, crossing his ankles to the front, and indicated its match opposite. Mackenzie sat, the deep cushions molding to the contours of his long frame, providing instant comfort. Duke moved to stand next to his side, and with a click of Mack's fingers, the dog sat, back rigid, head held poised.

"Pedro never mentioned any associate to our...er...business," Thorn said, flicking his gaze from the dog back to Mack. "I wonder how you came to make the connection."

"We likely didn't know of each other at the time." Mackenzie pulled air through his nose, then licked his lips. "In light of your recent loss, I won't waste your time. I will do you the respect you so obviously deserve." He lifted an arm to indicate the opulence of the room. "You have information I require in order to continue my journey. I come equipped to reward your assistance."

"And will the good Captain Alvarez also be paying me a visit?"

Mackenzie stroked Duke between the ears and didn't rush the answer. "I think not."

"I see," Thorn said as a plate of finger sandwiches arrived, and Donnelly laid the small table. Once the butler departed, neither reached for food. Instead, Thorn drained the amber liquid in his glass. "And if I could compensate you for your portion of the information?"

Mack's hand stalled on Duke's ear. The dog turned his head to stare at his master. He forced a smile and patted the dog, then picked up his crystal goblet. "One is nothing without the other," he said vaguely. "That is true. And it seems I was misinformed in assuming there was a deal to be had."

Thorn replaced his glass on the tabletop with a thud. While he inclined his gaze, his fingers drummed a beat on the arm rest. "'Tis truly an impasse."

Chapter Five

By the time Flora shooed—pushed—threatened—away the more regular waterfront girls from their spot, leaving one with a blackened eye for her effort, she'd lost sight of her mark. Damn—and more colorful words—pushed their way up her throat as she elbowed another from her staked location. The tall man with the confident air had the look of one newly minted. Captain or an officer, for sure. He had the swagger only a full purse could produce.

This only made her angrier when another sea whore sidled up to claim the lamppost as her own. Used to rough living, Flora never hesitated to punch, bite, and spit as necessary. She took the measure of her competition. At the moment, holding the spot seemed counterproductive to attracting someone. That is, until she spoke.

"This 'ere's our piece," the girl said, battering Flora with a boney hip. To an outsider, the move may have looked as though they were having a bit of fun. But the girl, one Flora gauged to be of an approximate age as she, had hips as sharp as slate rocks, and she had wielded them with enough force to off balance Flora.

Grazing her hands and knees in the fall, Flora bounded to her feet in a fury. Without missing a beat, she socked the girl in the gut and laughed uproariously as though they were " 'aving a bit 'o fun" before thrusting her into the milling crowd. "Not today."

That had been two long hours ago. Unable to find another decent mark, and having no intention of fulfilling the role of prostitute, Flora gazed around the steady mob, ready to admit the defeat. The unaccustomed flounced skirts were too cumbersome for her usual pickpocket routine. Resigned, she sighed. Puffing her cheeks, she decided she'd recount the coin tonight. Perhaps Maggs had been right and she had enough money already to finally leave Halifax behind. Still, Flora had been taught to be pragmatic and would have preferred a cushion for those just-in-case moments Maggs had always drilled into her.

Deciding to leave, she'd yet to determine where to go. Sure, Maggs always envisioned returning to England, but to what? Flora couldn't imagine a different life there from the one she already had. She had no known relatives, and her money would only take her so far. One city to another made no never mind if she'd end up the same. Better the devil you know, if that was going to be the case, and save the money. No. She pinched the bridge of her nose. She had to think this through.

Posters along Water Street this morning confirmed the authorities were looking for the boy who'd been seen often with the whore Maggs. Flora had to keep reminding herself of her get-up and how someone would have had to know her to connect the two.

Distracted, she stepped away from the post. An immediate replacement staked her claim. Flora cast her gaze around the waterfront and shrugged. Then an abrupt, nauseous bile rose up in her throat. She had to contain the urge to run. Instead, she locked her quavering knees, placed a hand on her hip, and swaggered a few feet into the throng.

Across the width of the pier, tall enough to be seen above the sea of peddlers, the lantern-jawed man Maggs had robbed and Flora had kneed in the bollocks hassled some of the venders. There could be no mistaking those distinctive features. This was the man Flora had assumed from the rumblings to be called Cain, the dead son of Tommy Two-Guns. So if the living form survived, who was Cain and how had she and her mother been blamed for his death?

She squeezed her eyes closed, then re-opened them. Perhaps she only conjured him. There he stood. Not dead at all. Questions rolled over one another as she tried not to stare and draw attention. Certainly, she'd heard the cop tell the other that Tommy Two-Guns' son had died and she and her mother were supposedly responsible. How else would they have gotten the unique knife, inscribed with his initials and found with her mother's body, if not off Cain himself?

Lantern Jaw with the roving eyes wove through the crowd, scowling as much as laughing, depending on who he encountered. As she listened, she heard him respond to the name "Billy Seconds," who appeared to be well known amongst the locals.

Who then killed Cain? Did she care? Emotions reeled in contest. Two-Guns' son being alive or dead wouldn't bring her mother back. Cold, deprivation, consumption, and a shot to the ribs by this brute had claimed Maggs. But as they were still looking for Flora, or more accurately the boy who accompanied Maggs, she'd care. They'd want her. They'd want someone to pay for the son's death, and who better to take the fall than gutter rats?

Could this Billy Seconds recognize her in her present costume? At that moment, the man locked eyes with her, his fish-eyed stare bore into her, and if possible the muscles of his jaw tightened and thrust his bottom lip forward.

Flora struggled not to drop her gaze, swayed her hips, and forced a grin to lift her cheeks. Today, she'd taken on the role of the doxy. She'd seen Maggs perform enough; she'd be able to assume the moves. But blood pounded in her ears so loudly she watched his lips move as he approached, yet she couldn't hear the words.

Suddenly the man guffawed and nudged a seaman ambling by. "Dumb as a stump, this one."

"That's for the best, mate," the marine replied in a thick, barely recognizable accent. "You're not paying for chatter."

"Too right you are," Billy Seconds agreed. "Too right."

The bluejacket passed by, and Flora thought she might collapse at any moment with the effort to remain where she stood. Billy Seconds seemed interested and stood still, his head tilted to the side as he continued to eye her instead of passing on.

"Well, what you lookin' at?" She forced the brazen words out past stiff lips, laying on an accent parroted from another of the wharf workers. "You either buyin' or movin' on."

She shouldn't have spoken, Flora realized too late. Despite the effort to disguise her own vocals, her face, cleaned of soot, mirrored her mother's, never mind the red hair. Self-consciously she lifted a hand to fluff the short curls under the bonnet.

His brow dropped low over his fish-round eyes, which deepened into their crevices while his mouth puckered. "What you say?"

Flora folded her lips into a thin line and crossed her arms over her slight chest, the weighty material pooling in the front. Unlike the breeks and jacket she normally wore, the dress made her feel exposed and vulnerable. Still, she refused to answer. She'd provide no second chance to recognize her voice. Leave him to wonder.

"She don't know what's about," said the girl Flora had recently socked in the guts. Hips swaying, she ambled up to Billy to stroke her fingers along his bulging bicep. "She ain't never been 'ere afore t'day. If you's lookin' for a good time, sweet'art, you let ol' Cora be the one for you, sweet'art."

Billy flung Cora's arm off and pierced her with a menacing stare. A frisson of small pleasure coursed through Flora when she saw the hustler take a step back.

He stepped closer to Flora and sniffed. "Never been 'ere afore, eh?" He cast his gaze back to Flora. "Where's you been, then?"

Flora held the silence for as long as she dared. When he refused to move on, she bit the inside of her cheek. When he bent at the waist to come so close she could smell the morning ale on his breath, she wrinkled her nose and blurted, "Don't be listenin' to that trash." She lifted her chin toward Cora. She'd spoken on impulse. She spread her stance, bracing herself, readying to pounce or run, based on his response.

His brow lifted, and she realized her mistake. Out of habit, she had lowered the tenor of her voice, and she had no doubt this time he recognized her—if not the look of her, certainly the sound of her.

Quick as a snake, meaty fingers grabbed her face and clenched under her jawline. He brought his face close so their noses almost touched. Mead, sausage, and onions assaulted her nostrils. "I know you."

Flora's eyes darted from side to side. Cora had disappeared, and she'd receive no assistance in this crowd of fish mongers, peddlers, and merchant sailors. Altercations were not rare, but plentiful and expected, as she knew quite well. She'd have to run and cursed the bulk of the dress, which would impede her escape. A good head start would help. If only she could hoist her knee up through the bulk and force a loosening of his muscled embrace.

Flora met Billy's stare and tried to smile to soften the violence emanating from his every pore. His thumb and forefinger pressed so tightly into her cheeks she felt her molars rub the lining.

"Oi. Speak, my little canary."

Billy hoisted her higher, stretching her neck, leaving her no choice but to rise on her toes. Lips pulled back revealed the broken incisor. His eyes roamed her face, and with his free hand, he flung back the bonnet.

"What 'appened to your hair, sweeth'art?"

His tone had taken on a jovial note she found more menacing than a growl. She felt rather than saw him moving her through the crowd away from the crush. Her vision had narrowed, with a white fog shrouding the edges. Though she gripped his corded wrist and dug her nails, she could gain no purchase. She tiptoed to keep pace in order to retain the little airflow allowed. If she dropped her weight, his hand would clamp her neck entirely.

"You've got something of mine, and I'd like it back," he hissed into her ear and bit the lobe. "Only thing they found with that whore was a knife. No money. No purse. No—"

She couldn't concentrate on his words. Gibberish. Instead, with all her might, Flora rounded her fist, thumb knuckle leading, and swung her hand into Billy's neck.

"Ugh," he exploded as unexpected air and spittle released into Flora's eyes.

When he loosened his hold, she hoisted her skirts and, bracing against his shoulders, kneed him. She missed her mark and connected with his upper thigh. With no more time to waste, seeing they were so close to the alley, she grabbed her heavy folds of skirt and took flight down the mildew-greased corridor.

Mist had begun and the already slippery cobbles became treacherous. She slipped, fell, crawled, got up, and ran again.

"Not this time," Billy growled as he lunged to catch the back of her trailing dress.

He flung her, feeling weightless, against the wall, and air abandoned her body with the impact while her head bounced off the bricks. Sparks flew in her vision, and her head felt like a ship unmoored from the rest of her body. Her vision narrowed to a tunnel. All her expectations of this moment led her to one conclusion...he would kill her, and with Maggs gone, no one would help or care. Did anyone even know her name? Her full name—Florence Marie Rivers.

"Where's the map?" Billy had his hand wrapped around her windpipe again, applying subtle but insistent pressure.

She couldn't shake her head, and her hands dangled at her sides. Air wheezed through her lips. "I don't—"

"Not so mighty on your own, now, are ye?" Spittle marked hot against her cheeks while the mist continued to fall. "Ol' Two-Guns had me an' some others go over that hole you crawled outta and found nothin' but Cain's knife. So…where'd you stash it, eh? Where's me map?"

It? Map? What? Flora wobbled her head in an attempt to indicate a negative answer. He'd tightened his grip to the point where even words couldn't pass.

Billy shook her, and flesh and bone collided with uneven bricks. The waft of metal accompanied the hot trickle of blood over her shoulder. "You may 'ave spent the money, but I want me map back. That's where my fortunes lie."

Flora felt her eyes grow larger, drying with the lack of blinking as they bulged with his insistent grip. Her vision seemed to reach for the air her lungs could not grasp. *This is it, then*, she surmised. She'd be with her mother soon. Not so bad. Her father and brother too. The thought almost comforted her. Almost. If not for the notion that she'd have to spend an eternity knowing this grunt of a man, Billy, was the cause of her demise.

Assembling the last of her reserves, she clenched her numbed fingers and lashed out with her fists. When this seemed to have little to no impact, she raked him with her nails, feeling the trenches she gashed from his ear, along his jaw line.

"Uh," he breathed. "You little bitch."

He loosened his vise-like grip long enough for her

to draw breath before he again slammed her against the wall. A crazed gleam took hold in the dark depths of his fish-orbed eyes, and she understood he had lost control and there would be no going back from his intent to harm, if ever there was a chance. They had bypassed revenge and gone straight on to vengeance when he pushed his knee between her knees and began to haul her skirts up.

"Like that, is it," he growled between clenched teeth and pinched her upper thigh. "I'll teach you a lesson."

Just as Flora felt her eyes roll up and darkness begin to consume her, a vicious growl came from deep within the tunnel of her existence. Had Pa's dog gone along to heaven with him? Then she felt her body go limp and free as she floated to the sodden ground. She'd been released. All of her weight fell away, and she drifted, wondering if heaven would look like the farm they'd once had.

Chapter Six

The familiar scent of brine, sludge, and unwashed bodies alerted Flora to the fact that she wasn't going to heaven today. Or if she was, the preacher had certainly misinformed the congregation about paradise. Perhaps her lack of good deeds would prevent entry in any case. In her memory, the farm never reeked like this, and certainly God would take better care of the eternally saved.

Her nose quivered, and she understood she could breathe. Her lungs felt tight and her throat constricted, but the effort of drawing air in and out was evidenced by the motion of her chest, which she felt under her crossed fingers where they lay. By some miracle, she remained alive. Each small movement caused a buzz along her limbs, tingles to the tips of her fingers.

Still unwilling to acknowledge her re-emergence into a life she'd rather leave behind, she kept her eyes closed and her body still. The lantern-jawed Billy could be hovering close by, and why take a chance when she didn't know what she was getting back into. Just what had happened? She squeezed her knees together. Did she want to know? Her head ached like it had been kicked around by horses and the hooves had left their mark.

Nausea threatened to give her away. Her stomach had started to lurch. Any moment she would retch. That she remained on the docks was apparent in the thick bouquet of sweat, shit, and general oppression. But something pleasant hovered as well. She flared her nostrils. Very close by hovered the tantalizing scent of soap and some sort of spice.

"Jesus, Capt'in, we can't take a doxy on board."

Her ears perked at the unfamiliar tones. Certainly not the British or French she was used to. She'd been found by a captain. Could this be true? What luck cast her upon this mark? Maggs would be pleased by the notion. Flora could almost smile imagining her mother's face, but the smallest movement caused her to ache all over. Still, at least for the moment, no one was trying to strangle and rape her. If she lay still long enough, perhaps she'd gather enough strength to run.

"Of course not," replied a deep masculine voice. There was a near chuckle on the edge of the tone. "Make no mistake, this lass 'ere's no doxy."

The rustle of air preceded his man's "Eh?"

"Look at 'er," the captain drawled, and the smell of fresh air wafted closer. "The lass is trying too hard to pass."

"I could do with a doxy a-trying."

"Couldn't we all." He released a laugh, which ended as abruptly as it had begun.

The captain's chortle, so pleasant, warmed the penetrating chill of the rocks beneath her shoulders. Deep and throaty, with just a hint of lust Flora couldn't help but hope she initiated. Her mother certainly had that ability to draw out such reactions in men. It had kept them from starving, and as Maggs often said, there was no shame in that.

"You need a woman," the first voice said with a

snort. "Christ, we all need a woman. They be plenty about. Better than this snip of a girl. Getcha one with hair, at least."

A grunt followed.

"And a bosom. Now that you say it, I agree. I don't think she be a doxy a-tall. That hair and no bosom? Dirty and smelly? Least ways a prostitute does try. Could be a fella in disguise. They do that, you know. Some prefer—"

A dog barked, and Flora jumped. The movement caused white-hot pain to slice through her skull. She coughed, and the movement spasmed, constricted air flow. Her hands reached to thread either side of her neck and hold the contents in place.

"There now," said the deep voice of the captain. He sounded so calm, while she thought life would drain away at any moment. "I thought you'd come around."

"What happened to that dirty bastard?" she croaked, not yet ready to face the world. "He's supposed to be dead."

A cool hand touched her throat, and she flinched.

"I think you're proof he's very much alive," he said, pulling his hand back. "That'll take a while to heal. You'll be bruised, for sure."

The voice melted over her like the butter she'd seen put on fresh bread she and Maggs could never afford. The common-sense side of her brain screamed caution, yet she couldn't deny the comfort of his presence. Safe. A condition Flora had not known in years—if ever.

A thought entered her reviving mind. She couldn't yet focus her blurred vision. Still, this captain sounded well fed and educated. If she played the situation up, she could come out of this further ahead than she had anticipated this morning.

"I'm sure you work better under the cloak of darkness, for I am no mark," he said, voice harder, gravelly. He spoke as though possessed of the ability to surmise her intentions as they appeared in her head. Then he huffed. "Yes. Everything you think shows on your face, and you're too young and obviously too lacking in experience for this life."

She stiffened. Then as his words penetrated, Flora snorted—and winced with the pain of the action. She covered her flaming cheeks with her palms. "Ye know nothin' about me life."

Flora heard the rustle of cloth, smelled the wet wool, and opened her eyes to focus on her savior. Stooped at the waist, hat held in one hand, he held the other out to her.

"Come on now," he said, deep blue-black eyes boring into hers. A massive scar scored the side of his handsome, swarthy face. "As you say, I know nothing about your life, but my dog here did save it."

As though on cue, the dog barked again, causing her to quickly gain her feet. Her gaze swept to the gigantic black beast sitting next to the captain's leg, mouth open and panting, revealing very large teeth. The massive head stood level with the captain's bent elbow. His ears were perked, and his tongue lolled slightly, and her heart calmed its riotous tattoo.

"'Tis a bear," she gasped, her free hand cradling her neck where it ached more than the other parts of her body.

The captain didn't release her hand but smiled down at her, his dark eyes crinkled at the edge in a weathered face. "That's Duke, and though big, he's not as large as a bear."

Flora gawked. When she flicked her gaze back to the captain, she recognized him from that morning. She must be unsteady on her feet, because his other hand clasped her shoulder, his hat tapping against her back.

"Steady she goes," he said, scanning her features. "You're pale, but that may be your natural coloring. I know not."

Flora felt the flush rise like a fire being stoked. She shook her head, regretting the action instantly, and then looked around more cautiously. They stood away from the hordes still milling in the main body of the waterfront. He must have carried her there. Out at anchor she spied the sleek ship she knew belonged to this enigma of a man. Had she not marked him that very morning as his man pulled the long boat in and then returned to the ship sitting high above the water line? Perfect for her intention. A ship recently divulged of its wares meant men with money to spend. Men like him, with loose coin heavy in their pockets. A chicken waiting to be plucked.

"Not me, lass," the captain broke into her thoughts. "I told you, I'm no mark."

Bloody hell. She stamped her foot. "Stop doing that," she said, complaint evident in her tones. "You're not allowing me to say thank you."

"He's never wrong, lass," his man said, coming up beside her. "He's the gift of a witch, he has. Calls him Black Mack, and he's our protection out a-sea."

"That's enough of that. Superstitious codswallop," the captain said, holding a palm up, the lashing scar adding more authority to his words. "No need to scare the girl."

Flora cast the seaman a withering glare, noting with surprise the ruddy cheeks on a scrubbed face with the snaggletooth smile. She wasn't used to such cleanliness. "Better beware of fires then," she spat, turning to face the captain. Noticing her hand still engulfed in his, she drew out of his grip. "Stay out of my head."

"She's a feisty one," the mariner said.

"That she is," said the captain, standing to his full height, which put him a full head over his man. His wide eyes now seemed more bright than threatening, with a delicious fire in their depths. "And seems quite recovered. We will leave you, then."

With an inclination of his head, a smile still hovering on his full lips, and a flick of his fingers, he stepped back and then turned. The dog and the man followed as a unit and moved toward the longboat roped to the side of the wharf.

Flora watched the man walk away and felt a strong tug that something important had evaded her grasp. Her mother's wish for Flora to escape this hellhole came back to her in the flurry, each word like a blow in her pounding head. A reminder that no one here on the harbor front would have missed her had she died at the hands of Billy Seconds propelled her forward.

"Wait," she called, just as the dog leapt down to the sloop rolling in the tide.

The captain turned, his face a friendly mask she couldn't read. Flora hoisted her skirts and ran after him. "Take me with you."

The captain placed a fist on his hip, the other held in a stop motion to his man and Duke. Then he turned his hooded gaze back on her. "I beg your pardon?"

"'Tis your ship yonder." She lifted her chin and pointed toward the horizon. "I need to get out of here. He's supposed to be dead, Tommy Two-Guns' son." She racked her brain to recover the name. "Cain, is he?" She nodded, acknowledging the correct memory. "And now they do for me, as they did me ma. That big bastard was just the beginning."

Though the captain's brow crinkled, he did add a comment. His tongue peeked out between his lips, and he traced a hint of moisture over the cracks. He lifted a booted foot to the lip of the dory and leaned an elbow down upon his knee.

In the gulf of his interested silence, Flora pressed on. "Me ma, Maggs as she was known, passed just yesterday, and we was blamed for the killing of that man who attacked me, or so I thought. But no, it wasn't him but this fella Cain, Two-Guns' boy."

"And did you?"

"Did I what?" she asked, stepping close to the edge of the wharf.

"Kill the man?"

"No, 'course not." She looked over her shoulder, back to the crowds dwindling now that the day's market was almost at an end. "You saw yourself that he did for me."

The captain shook his head, and Flora couldn't help the flow of the words. She couldn't stay here. The bruising on her throat was a reminder of how she wasn't ready to join the rest of her family.

His gaze narrowed, and he placed his hat upon the dark curls. "I'm sorry for your loss, lass." He inclined his head briefly, tilting his hat. "But as you say, he's no more dead than you are, so your ma, God rest her soul, is cleared, and so shall you be."

Flora shook her head vigorously. "No. No," she gasped, losing the bit of breath she'd been able to hold in her lungs. "Tommy Two-Guns' son is still dead. I thought it be he who attacked me, but as you say, not so. But Two-Guns' son Cain still be dead, and they be a-blaming Maggs and me. I think…" A sudden thought sprang into reality. "What if it be he who killed Cain and came after me and Ma to blame?"

The captain pivoted the palm he'd held up to the dog toward Flora. "I'm sorry for your trouble, lass. 'Twas unplanned on my part to get involved," he said with a swift glance at his dog. "I blame Duke for that. But a ship…my ship…any ship…is no place for a lass. So unless you have the other half of the map I seek, you have no further value."

He'd spoken offhand, but the words rang. Billy Seconds had said the same. A map. "Where me fortunes lie," was what he'd said before her sight had blurred.

With another incline of his head, the captain stood, brushed his pants, and indicated his man to maneuver out from amongst the other sloops. As she watched, he stood commandingly in the center, the sway and spray of the waves from the tide unable to unbalance him.

Into Flora's memory, on the heels of the remembered words, sprang the image of the wad of leather with the writing. She didn't allow herself time to doubt as puzzle pieces aligned.

A man like this in Halifax harbor on business. The biggest man in town being Tommy Two-Guns. She and Maggs had robbed Billy Seconds, who worked for Two-Guns as the money man. If Billy killed Cain,

Tommy's son, and stole the map, which she and Maggs had then stolen from Billy…

Billy's words…"Where's my map?"

The boy hadn't yet laid his oars to water. Flora bent at the waist over the edge of the pier. "And if I did?" She placed her hands on his hips as she'd seen her mother do so many times. Her foot jutted to the side, giving her body a brazen angle. "Would you take me then?"

Chapter Seven

Mackenzie didn't like to tarry, but hadn't formulated what he'd tell his men to accommodate their questions when they didn't head out with the tide as originally planned. They were supposed to be at sea on their way with both halves of the map. Managing a ship's crew was a delicate balance of discipline and cajolery. This unexpected delay would have a ripple impact if not handled correctly.

"Judas priest," he cursed, pacing the upper deck. "God curse me if I'm taken for the fool by that snip of a lass."

Had the too-big-for-such-a-fragile-face eyes so easily persuaded him? Perhaps something of himself reflected in the green orbs. Someone struggling for their hold in this world often harsher and more unforgiving than the Bible would lead people to believe.

Still, he gripped the railing until his knuckles whitened. She had until sunup to produce the golden purse. Mackenzie almost trembled with the thought of having, by pure happenstance, come across the very item he risked port to procure.

"Not in hand yet," he reminded himself.

He would meet her on the rocks at McNab's launch. He'd made no promises and suspected an ambush, although there was no question she had been attacked. She knew Thorn's son's name and that he was dead. For all of her intent to perhaps roll him for any wealth in his pocket, her face had been a dead giveaway. No, he concluded his thoughts, marking her as truthful when she offered the map. Further, the bafflement, then glow which suffused her features put paid to her knowledge of what she possessed prior to his offhanded and, he chastised himself, careless remark.

It was a stretch, he knew, even as he related the adventure to Hemsley, who smiled wickedly. "By the blood. 'Tis worth the effort. Don't matter the how," he said, his gnashed teeth revealed in his grin, mere stumps along his gums. "Cheaper too, by far. We drop her at a port along the way. She's a new life. You did what you said you'd do, and we've the makin's afore being rich men…kindly supplied by that thievin' rogue, Blackbeard."

"Too true," Mack mused. "But she could be working for Thomas Thorn."

"That be a fact," Hemsley agreed, rubbing a thumb along the hilt of his blade forever strapped to his side. "But wouldn't be the first time for us, and…well, really makes no sense a-tall. If she be a workin' for Two-Guns, why then be his man a-goin' ta try an' kill her, as you say?"

Back and forth they worked the angles until both agreed, yes, meeting the lass was their only recourse. Never mind the luck of a woman on board.

"It be nothin' but luck you a-found 'er."

Mackenzie reached to scratch Duke between the ears and then under the great chin. "'Tis the great beast's fault."

"Well, there's no denyin' he always be lookin' out

for us," Hemsley said, his gaze trailing to the dog. "Saved me more than once, he did. No doubt he's doing the same now. I say, Duke likes the girl, then she be fine aboard."

And so he paced the hours away, unable to settle, unable to make a move until the dawn. Even Duke gave up the rigor of walking without destination and settled into his corner, dozing at intervals.

The sailors straggled back on board at all hours throughout the night in various conditions. Some beaten and bruised, bloodied and bedraggled, but all featured the beatific peace of men who'd had their fill of a much-needed release. This was a hard life they led, and a hard life they chose. With the change of the current, they'd regain the focus he needed for the next leg of their exploits.

After they secured the map.

Mack stared off to the purple-hazed horizon. No sign of the English patrol. Plenty of ships, men-o-war and the like, but none to have interest in his crew or cargo as high as they were in the waterline. Nothing to be gained.

As indigo paled into the bluish hue of fresh milk, he envisioned the sketch on the leather. He'd compared his etching to his many navigational charts and knew he'd find the island off the south of this New Scotland territory. But it was the entrance and where to begin that he was missing. He could only hope such was laid out in what he now gambled to secure, the pitfalls and the way through the labyrinth of decoys and artifice laid by that scoundrel Blackbeard to cheat others from finding the treasure. Surely, the man must have imagined taking it with him to whatever realm of hell he now commanded.

Mack shook his head, replaying his meeting with Thorn and how the man had pretended to still retain possession of the information. He recognized the artifice from this distance, what he should have seen when present. "Bloody hell," he cursed. Thorn hadn't been mourning his son as much as seeking what was lost to him. Now, Mack understood, he had a whole new enemy to contend with. All Mack had accomplished by approaching Thorn was to give away his hand that he had the other half. If Thorn had any wits at all, he'd identify the *Navigator* as a Spanish galleon formerly captained by Alvarez. Further, shouted Mack's frustrated brain, if Thorn waited, he'd also know when to strike to grab the treasure.

"Damn," he said, fist slamming against the rail. "God damn his eyes for threatening me."

"Sir?" the bosun questioned.

Mackenzie glanced over his shoulder and shook his head. "Nothing."

The bosun shrugged and turned to scan the horizon.

"Dawn's approaching," Mack barked. "Hemsley."

"Aye, sir?"

"All men aboard?"

"Aye, sir."

"Then set your course. You have your orders," Mack said, assuming his position at the quarterdeck. "There's a breeze freshening. Just enough to see us through."

"Aye, sir."

Before the violet pink of the sky had transformed to orange, the *Navigator* had rounded into position near the rocky bank.

Leaving Duke in his cabin, Mack called for the longboat, and he and Hemsley took their positions, Tiller at the oars. The boy was trustworthy and had more than proved his worth. They checked the priming of their firearms and stowed them within their holsters, then adjusted their swords at their hips.

"You know what to do, Tiller," Mack said, the statement more of a question.

"Aye, Capt'in."

Mack cast a superstitious glance back to his ship, Burke's stocky form easily visible, alone with a few mariners standing watch, waiting for his signal. If he needed to signal.

The beach sat deserted at this hour. Even the fishermen weren't yet about. This did little to assuage his anxiety. In his experience, empty usually left a multitude of eyes watching. His boots crunched on the rocks as he stepped from the boat through the shallows and onto the shore. A hand at his hip ready to grab his pistol, Mack nodded to Hemsley and Tiller to remain on alert and in the sloop. Mack caught the glint of steel in Hemsley's hand and breathed easier.

Within the span of a few racing heartbeats, movement captured his attention. From the treeline, a slight body scurried along the edge, keeping low to the ground. Only a woman had such grace. A new thud added a different rhythm to the staccato of his pulse.

Smart, he thought. If he opened fire, she'd likely get away, lost in the foliage.

There was an elegance about her progress toward him. For a fleeting breath he wondered if she'd been misplaced. Someone fallen on hard times and not really meant for the life she currently led? She'd shed the ridiculous costume of the day before. With no heavy flounces to impede her, she moved swiftly and with intent, a small sack bouncing off her shoulder.

He realized with a start he didn't even know her name. They'd bargained, and he hadn't so much as asked her name. Before he could castigate himself further, she was across from him with less than fifty yards separating them, she standing willowy in the treeline and he as stout as the rocks on the beach. The longboat floated another equal distance away in the shallows.

"I have what you want," she called. Small curls had escaped her cap to frame her face.

"Allow me to inspect it, then."

Her brows dipped, and she pulled her bottom lip between her teeth. She swayed, and he realized she bounced from foot to foot as though preparing for flight. Then she stopped, released her lip, and her stare cut sharply across the distance. "You'll take me with you."

She wasn't asking, he realized. There was command in her tones, and he bit back a bark of laughter at the audacity.

"If it is what you claim."

Her hesitation showed no unease, just someone weighing the odds. Mack recognized this as something he too would do in such a situation. She must be contemplating whether he was her best option. Surely, she could sell it to Thorn. He'd already surmised as much. Yet by this point she'd know that without the match each piece on its own was close to useless. No, he allowed a small smile, she'd been gripped by curiosity. She wanted to see this to the end.

Yes, he confirmed, he could shoot her and be done. He'd have the map and be off with no further burden to contend with or need to explain away. From this vantage, she offered a solid target, and he was a quick shot, but Mack found himself intrigued. He too wanted to see where this new development led.

She stood, and he watched her glance from him to the sloop and out farther to the *Navigator*. "Take me to your boat and I will give it over." She stepped one pace closer.

He mirrored her movement, drawing closer by one step. "When I have what I seek, a bargain will be struck."

She shook her head, glanced over her shoulder, then along down the beach, her hands balling into fists at her sides. "How do I know you'll not rob me and leave me where I am?"

"Or worse," he said, keeping his voice light but clear. A sudden image of her writhing body beneath his, taking pleasure from his skills, distracted his attention. "I could easily take what I want and leave."

At his words, she had retreated into the trees, the foliage easily obscuring her slight figure clad in the guise of a lad. Then she shook her head and stepped firmly back on the rocky bank. "No," she said. "You coulda killed me yesterday."

Although he'd not mentioned death, he could understand her concern. "Yes," he replied, fighting to keep the chuckle from his tones, reminding himself she could be baiting him. Perhaps he should have sought a doxy for himself. Then he wouldn't find himself so distracted by a snip of a barely formed woman. "But yesterday you had nothing of value worth taking. Today is a different story."

A blast of curses flowed over the breeze to him, and this time he didn't hold back the chortle. He had no tingle of threat, and he had learned a long time ago to trust his instincts. Whatever concerns he may have had had vanished with the morning mist. On that note, he waved back at Hemsley and stalked across the rocks toward the girl without a name.

At his approach, her chin lifted, though her sight altered like a pendulum between him and his men. Then, to his surprise, she set one determined foot in front of the other, matching him pace for pace until they ate the distance between them.

"If we were dueling, we're walking in the wrong direction," he commented as they came face to face.

At the confusion on her face, he waved a hand and shook his head. Her green eyes glinted, and he wondered how he had missed their extraordinary color yesterday. Must have been the dusk, dirt, and circumstance. Today, although clad in rags, threadbare and loose-fitting, she was significantly cleaner, with next to no reeking scent compared to the stench from the day previous.

"You'll take me with you as promised?"

She'd be a dangerous addition on his ship should the men suspect a woman—willing or no—no matter the prize promised.

He stared down at her, her upturned face, reaching barely to his breastbone. "I didn't promise," he corrected. The cropped hair did little to distract from the pearl satin of her skin, the fine bone structure which showed a woman of quality. "I said I would meet you to see what you had."

The round eyes stared unblinking, while her face fell. She looked on the verge of tears, and his heart constricted. He didn't doubt the truth of her words when she said she'd just lost her mother. He knew his own heartbreak when he found his mother had died, and he hadn't seen her in years at that point.

"There now," Mack said, voice softer, curling his hands into a fist to prevent himself from touching her. "Let's see what you have, and we'll strike a bond."

She stared up at him, full bottom lip caught in a tremble. Her clear eyes offered a mirror to the inner workings of her mind. She had no one, of that he was positive. And she was young. Much younger than his twenty-four. "How old are ye, lass?"

Her chin shot up again before she answered. "Eighteen and a hard worker," she said. "I can turn my hand to anything."

He considered her failed attempt at prostitution, and this generated an obscene glee that she hadn't succeeded in the profession. He mentally shook the thought. What she did to survive didn't involve him.

"I'm sure you can," he said with a nod. "Now, show me the map, and allow me to be on my way…with or without you."

****

Sloshing through the small currents, Mack strode toward Burke, fighting hard to keep his step measured so as not to give away his almost overwhelming excitement. By rote, Mack checked the course and the lee of the wind. The coastline would remain a companion on the horizon, but with the wind in their sails, they wouldn't be long before they were out to sea.

He stared into the middle distance. In the clarity of

hindsight, Mack relived the moment he saw his plan coming together. As soon as she pulled out the strip of leather, he'd recognized it at once as the companion to his own. On the beach, he didn't dare touch it. The tremble of his fingers couldn't be trusted. He needed all his wits. Though she may not be a doxy, he'd no doubt of her adaptability as a thief. He'd marked her as a pickpocket. Not that he blamed her, but if she understood the value...where it led...

"What are you called?"

She straightened to her full height. "My name's Florence," she said, and there was that quality again. Something that marked her as misplanted. Then it was gone. "But I'm called Flora."

She sat awkwardly on the bench in the longboat. She swayed as though she were going to fall over the side at any moment. Clearly, she was afraid, and he imagined this to be her first time in a boat, never mind surrounded by men who could at any moment slash her throat. She held her fear in check, and he again admired the strength of anyone, never mind a woman, capable of such a feat.

The bruising on her neck glowed, and Mack had a sudden urge to kill the son of a bitch called Billy Seconds for daring to touch such a beauty. His thought shocked him.

"Maggs called me Sam during the day." She lowered her chin and with a sweep of her hand indicated her outfit. "Maggs was me ma."

"Ah."

They had yet to start rowing back to the *Navigator*. Mackenzie cast a glare at the other three in the boat, meeting first Hemsley's eye, then Tiller's. "Outside of

Burke, her identity remains a wayward scamp we picked up who will offer a use on our mission," he said, his tone dark, brooking no resistance. "Sam it is, then."

Flora smiled, her face alight, and he scowled, wondering how she'd ever passed as a lad.

"Don't ever smile aboard my ship," he commanded, his jaw tight and teeth clenched. He turned to Burke. "Christ Jesus, I'll have a mutiny on my hands, each one expecting a piece o' her. She'll be under your protection."

"Aye," he said with a nod.

Tiller picked up the oars and, with a slight assent of his head, Mack allowed the boy to strike off for the ship.

At his gruff words, she had pushed back on the bench and almost toppled backward. Mack reached out swiftly to grab her by the shoulder, his hand lingering a bit too long. He coughed and moved to stand at the bow, the sway not impeding his own balance.

In moments, certainly not long enough for him to be convinced by his own plan, they'd bumped against the *Navigator*.

"Maggs wanted me to return to England," Flora said, her fingers wrapped tight around the edge of the bench, knuckles white.

"Have you family there?"

"None as I know," she said, looking up at him though her head remained bent, her cap shadowing her features. "She just wanted me outta here." She lifted her chin and focused on the beach beyond. A sour-smell look made her features fall.

"I see." Why he would be moved by such information baffled him, since he too had no family to speak of. Nor, given time and circumstance, was that unusual. Most of his crew could claim the same. Why then did his heart weep a small bit for her?

He swept the thoughts away once they reached the ship, and he grabbed the rope ladder. Striding to the quarterdeck, he skimmed the charts, then pointed. "Set your course, Hemsley. We've our destinations waiting for us."

"Aye," the man said before yelling orders to the crew.

****

"Steady as she goes, Capt'in," Burke responded to Mack's unspoken question two hours later.

"What of the lass, Burke? What's being said?" Mack asked as he pulled his spyglass from his breast pocket and put it to his eye to scan the horizon to the port side of the ship. The day was warm, and a trickle of sweat slithered the length of his spine. They'd be a day at most to their destination, within two turns of the tide, and he was no closer to knowing what to do about the girl.

He inspected the now whole map, matched hers to his own, and the thrill in his blood had set a new pace for his heart. He felt like he'd been to battle and back. His fingers still tingled from where they touched the leather and overlaid it with his own navigational maps to make a complete and up-to-date drawing of what they were going into.

"By the blood," he muttered. If the legends held true, this haul could set them for life. He'd get his fleet and make his enterprise legal—for the most part. He smiled. "I'll even buy a title."

"Ye means the lad, don't you, Capt'in?" Burke cut

across his fantasy.

Mack lowered the glass and contemplated the decking for a moment, suppressing a chuckle. He must stay focused. Too many distractions and all would be lost. "Ah. Yes, the new lad—Sam, is it?"

"That be he," Burke said while he scratched the stubble on his chin, not looking near as fresh as the day previous. "The young 'un… Sam's a scrawny lad, scrawnier even than the monkey Tiller, but seems willin' enough. As you suggested, he's to bunk off the kitchens by his self 'til he gets used to the way of the ship and all." Burke finished with a slight grin which formed a contrast to his normally haggard features.

Chapter Eight

The thick braid of coarse rope scraped across Flora's palm, burning. Flora—Sam as the sailors knew her—tried to secure a grip and failed again. Her fingers gave like twigs. What looked so easy when the boy Tiller pulled and tied the lines as though they were thread in a silken shift, strained her hands, wrists, arms, and shoulders to the point she felt the limbs were being pulled from their very sockets.

Her ineptitude sent the sails flapping. Each gust crackled the sheets without catching the wind. "Judas," she gasped, aching to let go of the demon rope. Did she really suggest this as an idea, and did that dark hulk of a man agree?

"What's wrong with ye, lad," Clem, a one-toothed sailor screamed. His tattooed forehead pinched and blustered to puce. "Ye're soft. Christ almighty, give 'er over afore we sail in circles a-goin' nowhere."

Accustomed to rough living, street violence, and quite aware of the comings and goings of mariners on days ashore, their needs and the ease with which to pickpocket their drunken wealth, sober men at their duty left her ill prepared. Flora found her previous perceived toughness of little help in the current situation. Brains and tenacity were not equal to the basic brawn required for the rigors of life on board the *Navigator*.

Clem grabbed the line from her unresisting hands and shouldered her, none too gently, out of the way. When she stumbled but didn't move far enough, his ham-sized fist, darkened by stencils, sun, and salt, connected with the soft give of her chest. Flora careened but retained her feet on the swaying deck, instantly afraid she'd been found out already.

"Easy there, lads," the man Burke called in their direction. "We all remember our first days aboard."

Clem grunted and went about securing the line with expert precision and without a second glance until he tied the slip knot to the cleat at the base of the mast.

He cast his gaze toward the quarterdeck, confirming, as did Flora following his focus, that Burke had turned his back. "What in the bloody hell has the capt'in brought on board?" Clem wiped his palms on his billowing pants and shook his head, only the loose tail of hair swaying with the motion. "A favor to an old comrade, eh. We'll be droppin' ye right smartly overboard, ol' comrade or no, ye don't start pulling yur weight. I don't care what the master say." He tilted his chin toward the upper deck. "Now, away with ye and see if ye can make yursel' useful to the cook."

Flora nodded and scurried for the passage, keeping her head low. At least she wasn't vomiting. She'd heard a couple of sailors make wagers. The passage reeked with the stench of men living communally. Certainly not as bad as she first feared, as the captain— Mackenzie McGuire, she'd since learned his name— insisted the men bathe with the salt water after each shift and use a designated lavatory.

"Do for you too." Tiller had nudged her arm. "You had a fine ripe odor about you." He sniffed close to her hairline. "Better today, though."

Flora shoved him hard in the chest, feeling the heat rise in her face. She curled her fists, preparing to jab him, when he laughed so hard he bent double before loping away and up the mainsail mast to his nest in the wind.

Humiliated, and more by luck than actual memory of the location of the mess, she eventually lurched her way to the kitchen. Here at least she could understand the process. The great vats of food, though, were like nothing she'd ever before seen. How could the crew possibly eat so much?

"We's set aside a portion for ourselves, lad, else we get nothing," Dek, the cloudy-eyed cook, told her as she struggled to move the heavy pots into position. The first batch of men would arrive shortly for the midday meal.

"No way they'll finish this," she said.

"Sammy, me boy." Dek slapped her on the back, nearly knocking her to her knees with the impact. Dek spoke in a pigeon-English marked by his Spanish roots and too long at sea. "You'll see."

"Seeing" was something Flora didn't think Dek could do with the way his head constantly shook from side to side as though he were continuously trying to pull focus through the foggy orbs. But he knew his way around his kitchen.

"I should," he replied when she asked how long he'd been aboard as a means of learning more about the enigma of the captain. "I've been aboard since she was christened in Algeciras back in '53. I come aboard from a smaller sloop. Couldn't wait to turn my hand on a big 'un like this. I grew up a fisherman's son, but the meager fisher life not be for me."

Then he guffawed. "And certainly there be no priest's life for me."

"Those were your choices?"

His opaque gaze stared past her for a brief moment before he got back to mixing whatever concoction he planned for the men. "The sweet *Navigator*, that she be now, was my home when she be called the *Lion de Oro*. It not be the ship's fault of a distracted captain. When Capt'in Mack bested us and took her for his own, he kept me an' few others." Dek nodded his head in a means that seemed to reaffirm the facts to himself. "He be a good captain, and that be the truth."

He lapsed into a Spanish monologue Flora had no way of understanding. Head down, she kept to the duties she inferred.

Accustomed to settling for scraps, when it came time to eat, the food filled her stomach easily. Yet within hours, she found hunger assaulted her again after the hard labor of clean-up. Just when she thought they would be done, they replayed the exercise again for the evening meal.

"You'll do," Dek said when at last all pots, pans, and utensils had been washed and stacked and the fires banked for the night. His back to her, he hooked his hammock to pegs she hadn't noticed previously and rolled into the mesh, lacing his fingers behind his head and closing his eyes. "Don't forget the eggs. We start at four bells."

Flora didn't understand the request and decided not to question. She was supposed to know. Somehow, she'd find the eggs in the morning…somewhere. Flapping her fingers, too tired to reply, she dragged her tired limbs above to locate her assigned quarter. Little hampered her progress. She met with no one, only seeing the silhouette of the captain, and the great beast of a dog by his side, at the other end of her trek.

A mystery, that one, she thought, crossing the length of the ship. The scrap of leather—the Golden Purse, he'd called it in a whisper as he inspected it. Had she settled for too little? Hindsight revealed men willing to kill and a captain of a major vessel willing to do just about anything to get it. Still there was something more to him. She'd recognized the glint in his eye that morning on the beach. The very same many a man had focused on her mother, and the knowledge made her warm deep in her belly. Where had that glimmer gone now that she was worked like a mule on the water wheel? Perhaps she had imagined it.

The dark sky served only to remind her how weary she was, having never performed such labors before. A fine mist coated her face. The salt in the air tingled her tongue, and she licked her lips. The decks were barren of most of the men who'd taken leave of their daily tasks to do as Dek and roll into their bedding.

A frisson of nerves made her hesitate before going down below where Hemsley had indicated she'd be quartered when she first came on board. At the time, she hadn't bothered to question, relieved only to be on board and bound for somewhere—anywhere besides Halifax. But now her hand dithered before the latch. Playing at the boy never proved an issue, especially when young, but she'd never been required to do so for so long and surrounded by men. The acute protection offered by her mother's presence engulfed her with grief of that loss as well. Her fingers trembled and her legs weakened. Soon it wouldn't matter who was around, she'd be asleep where she stood. Mustering her fear, she opened the door.

A cluck echoed out of the dark when she unlatched the door. The aromas of hay and manure mixed with the acrid scent of tar and oak. Before closing the door, she reached for the flint and lit a candle stump. Flora lifted the light and stumbled back a pace. A goat bleated unconcerned before resuming his gnawing at the straw, while chickens clucked in their coops.

"Sweet Judas."

She didn't require further explanation. Though she had no notion of how to proceed, she recalled Hemsley's mention of the care of the animals. Then she laughed and closed the door. Certainly she would have no problem with the eggs.

"We'll figure it out together," she said, finding and spreading the hammock to the ceiling as she'd seen Dek do.

Chapter Nine

Flora woke abruptly when her shoulder connected with a solid, unmovable object. Had she not been in a hammock, she would have tumbled to the hay-strewn floor of the cabin. Unable to sit up, she held out her palms to fend off another attack of being battered against the wall. Blackness shrouded her. Bleats and clucks accompanied the creak and groans of the ship.

"'Tis the seven rings of hell," she said, managing to roll out of the netting and onto her knees, placing her hands over her ears. The pitch and heave removed her balance, and she collided with the goat.

Distant yells followed the moan and whistle of the wind through the cracks. She struggled to her feet, sudden fear stealing their strength.

"All hands." The bellow penetrated the wooden door. "Tie as you come."

The shout aroused the march of many feet scurrying overhead. What if the ship were floundering? She didn't understand the instruction. Flora had imagined her death many times over the years as she and Maggs avoided one narrow miss or another, but drowning had never been included.

Taking control of her breathing, she clenched her fists. Hooves thudded close to her ear. The goat had reared and narrowly missed. She felt for the door and escape.

Grasping the edge of the frame while the ship shook and shuddered, she turned back to the darkness. "Stay here," she said, re-latching the door behind her and wishing someone would say that to her so she didn't have to go above.

Terror gripped each step of her ascent. Her knuckles showed white where she gripped the railing. Surely this would be her death. Never in her life had she seen a storm blow so furiously and with such intensity. From the vantage point of land, a storm was a furious beast. On the deck of a ship, an insignificant speck on the boundless ocean, there was no shelter and no escape.

She opened the door to a world of chaos. The *Navigator* bucked beneath Flora's feet and she felt propelled into the air, lost in endless movement without boundary. Only the solidity of the deck, the shouts of ordered men accustomed to such events, and the wink of lamps provided any depth from which to measure her perspective in the darkness. A rope slapped her across the face and she understood.

Standing on wobbly knee joints, she forced the rope into a knot recently learned, proud when she tested its strength and it held. She scanned the area for the men, her feet leading her toward their shouts.

The sky proved indistinguishable from the sea, and both rained, ignoring the laws of gravity. Waves raged up, only to clap down like a fist seeking to pull something into its grip. Stinging pellets of water peppered from overhead, stinging shoulders, arms, each delivering a tiny prick, a bruise.

Flora had thought she knew cold before, but this bone-chilling damp when it was not even winter, combined with the taste of the sea in her mouth, wearied her beyond any expectations. Doing as she was told when she was told, she did the best she could, and no one took the breath to complain.

Her eyes grew accustomed to the gloom, and she came to understand dawn was breaking somewhere. Somewhere the sun shines now, she thought, tasting the metal of blood mixed with the salt. Only the heat of blood made her aware she'd been cut. Skin numbed from the chill and constant immersion meant she couldn't identify the location. If the ocean could be this freezing in June, what would the winter be like? She determined not to find out.

She'd thought she'd been frightened in the dark. The gray allowed her to see waves, larger than any building she'd ever seen, break over the side. As she cast her gaze aft, she marveled at how the captain held his ground at the helm, issuing orders as though he were pinned to the location.

More than once, a flood swept her footing aside and she felt the draw of the ocean. But tied as she was, the cable held her out of its embrace. Each time she was brought to her knees, by some miracle of survival she would rise again, grab the ropes, and continue doing whatever she was bid. Knowledge and experience didn't matter, only that she listened and obeyed.

At one point, Tiller stood beside her, a wide grin splitting his homely face. "'Twill all be over soon," he said, slapping her on the back. "The gash ain't so bad. Dek will sew ye up."

"Gash?" Her palm reached for her head, but she felt nothing but numbness. "The cook?"

"Cook and surgeon alike," he said. "Capt'in say

you must go below to help get grub. Just a ration of hard tack and beer 'til we're through 'ere."

"Through?"

"Off with ye. We're not to 'er eye yet." He pushed her toward the galley. "I's remember my first storm. 'Tain't nothin' so frightenin'.'"

Flora stumbled, following the momentum of the ship as he untied her, and looked back as she left the deck. "Does it get better?"

"Eh?" He wiped water from his eyes.

"The storms," she shouted to be heard, blinking against the sting of rain.

"Neh," he said, still grinning. "No, never do."

With a heave, she pushed the galley door closed against another crashing wave. Her hands were raw and bloody. As she turned, struggling to find her breath, a rag slapped against her face.

"Wipe yourself down," Dek yelled. "I'll not have ye bleeding all over. The men need their nourishment. Tie it if you must, and I'll get to you after the men are fed."

A great shudder shook the beams, and a crack like cannon fire sounded.

She bent over and covered her head.

"Eh, lad, that be just one of the holds. The men will get 'er right smartly," Dek said, clanging a wooden spoon against a cast-iron pan. "Get yur wits about ye now."

"Aye," she answered, propelled into action by the authority of his voice and the confidence that this was just another day at sea.

Then finally, after what seemed an eternity, the crew, by shifts, had been fed, the wounds tended, hers last, and they passed through the squall. Bone weary, there was no time for rest as they set about repairing the damage caused by the storm.

She learned as she stole above deck that they'd lost their spanker sail and the outer jib to the wind. Despite her fear, the hold was little impacted. She checked the animals, finally remembering the eggs, after Dek sent her to fetch them so "that goddamned rooster doesn't get lazy about his work."

Flora would have laughed, had she the energy.

The rooster and his harem seemed quite unperturbed by the storm Flora noticed upon her return. She gathered the eggs into the basket, careful to ensure each was separated by straw to avoid breakage in the sway of the ship, and made to return to the galley.

Looking up to the sails flapping in the swirl of the wind, she slipped on the slick deck and careened into a solid object.

"Judas," she said, making sure the basket and contents were unharmed.

"You'll do well to watch your step," the deep throaty voice of the captain said, his hands bracing her shoulders. "No need to fling yourself overboard before we reach our destination."

Flora stepped back, holding the basket close to her chest. Her skin burned where he touched. He offered the only warmth she'd encountered in hours. The very bulk of him seemed to shelter her from the elements. She didn't want to move.

"Is it always like that?"

His eyes crinkled at the edge, and the livid scar to the side, through his brow and ending at his temple, puckered. He lifted his cap before repositioning it in place, seeming to consider his answer, then smiled much like Tiller. "No."

"Thank Chri—"

"That actually wasn't bad. Some of the worst storms you'll ever encounter occur off by Sable Island, much farther out to sea," he said, his hands linking behind his back, the bounce of the ship seeming to have no ill effect on his balance and command of the vessel. "Many a ship's been lost out there. We're still relatively close to land, though we've blown off course a bit. But you've no need for concern."

His gaze held hers, so deep a brown as to appear nearly black, and she felt lost in his pull. In that moment, she could believe he had such command of the ship that a mere storm proved no match. The ship and crew seemed to melt away, and she had no wish to return to Dek or the galley or the bone-weary work, ever. "Why's that?"

But in the pause, he had turned and now strode away, either not hearing her or choosing not to answer.

Chapter Ten

"Judas priest," Mack cursed in a growl under his breath when Hemsley walked by and shot him a particular look. He'd made it to the quarterdeck, the listing back and forth having no impact at the moment. Had he really just touched another sailor? Bloody hell, of course he had. He'd broken his own rule, set when he agreed to bring this slip of a girl—barely a woman—on board.

Despite himself, he couldn't see the "boy" Sam. All he saw were the slight curves and womanly swell from the beach. The peek of red hair and bright, fluid eyes. No matter the bandaged head and rain-soaked clothes, he saw a fresh-scrubbed face and fair curls dancing in the breeze, catching the rays of the sun. Those round eyes, both defiant and hopeful but not scared, were windows to her very soul, he was sure. The courage of one willing to risk all to start again intrigued him...and this was precisely why women were a curse on ships.

Mack snapped his fingers to draw Duke to follow, then remembered he'd left the dog in his cabin for safety. Annoyed, he stalked to the helm and checked their course.

"Steady she goes," he bellowed.

"Aye," came a chorus of voices back down the line of command.

Then Tiller's high-pitched scream pierced the thick of clouds and rage of the wind. "Flagship astern…flagship astern."

Mack immediately turned to Burke to check the course and the maps, swiping the water from the waxed waterproof paper. He feared traveling this close to the coast, but they were freed from their cargo and ran the correct flags.

"No place to hide in this gale," Burke confirmed. "We'll be no good other than for matchsticks if we push closer. The waves will push us right into the rocks."

"Pray the storm provides its own cover," he returned, taking up his spyglass, blinking the rain from his vision. "If she hasn't spotted us, no need to draw attention by changing course. We've the proper markings. Give them no reason to perk curiosity. In this weather, we need only concern ourselves with keeping afloat."

"Right-o," Burke replied automatically.

Feeling the thrill of engagement, Mack returned the glass to his pocket, turned to check the lee, then the snap of the remaining sails set to capture the wind without taking on too much of the blast to either put them farther off course than they already were or threaten a capsize in combination with the increasing ferocity of the waves.

"Jumpin' Jesus!" Tiller yelled above the clatter. "She's spotted us and signaled us to halt!"

Mack pulled his spyglass again and made for the stern of the ship. Confirming Tiller's words, he strode to the main sail where the boy continued to sway like a monkey from the highest knot of ropes.

Mack braced a hand against the heavy oak. "Let

me know her every move," he yelled, craning his neck to look up.

"Aye, Capt'in," the boy returned, the sound almost lost with the shriek of the wind.

Returning to Burke, Mackenzie knew he could outrun the ship if he wanted. But he puzzled for a moment whether they might be flying false flags. That Tommy Two-Guns was a well-connected thug, of that Mack was sure, who hadn't gotten what he wanted from Mack's visit. For that matter, Mackenzie hadn't been what Tommy expected in the first place, since he wasn't a Spaniard. No, in his place, Mack wouldn't hesitate to follow, especially if he felt he'd been robbed.

Adding injury to Thorn's insult, Mack now had the whole map. It wouldn't take much for Tommy to put two and two together and come to check things out for himself. The treasure would be a trove, of that Mack was certain. If he'd been in Tommy's shoes, he'd certainly engage a crew to pursue. And what better opportunity than in the present weather? Another ship lost to the sea would raise no eyebrows, especially one of dubious repute and during a storm.

Mack paced the deck heedless of the rough and pounding water which swept others off their feet. They had nowhere to hide, but he wasn't about to let the unknown pursuers board the *Navigator*.

Well, to their own peril, if they persisted in pursuit.

"All hands on deck," Mack yelled, and word flew around the ship. "Take your positions and have the guard ready the guns."

"Ready the guns?" Oscar, a ball boy, asked the tall, lanky man next to him who stood within hearing distance of Mack. "What the 'ell do ye mean 'ready the guns?' In this weather, they'll leap straight into the ocean and take us with 'em."

Mack flew across the deck. "Better you pay a visit to ol' Davey Jones than let a rival board what's ours."

Fear engulfed the seaman's face. "Aye," he said, bowing his head and setting to his duty.

Mack returned to Burke's side and shouted orders. With a sudden shudder that had him grabbing the line to hold his position, the *Navigator* fought against the pull of the ocean as the ship changed her course. Above, Tiller swung from the ropes, flying like a flag before wrapping his legs around the mast above the taut canvas.

The wind gusted and threatened to remove Mack's tricorn hat. Loose curls blew about his face, slapping his cheeks like tiny whips. But he paid no attention. In for a penny, in for a pound. As they moved out of the eye and farther into the storm, he knew this night he had two opponents, the ocean and the rival ship. One or both might win, but he intended to be the victor over both, and by tomorrow, he'd be at Oak Island ready to pursue the treasure.

The sky blackened rapidly, matching his mood. The crew heeded his orders while all the time keeping a ready eye on their opponent. It came as a great relief he'd admit only to himself when Tiller shouted from the foremast that the ship had turned.

"Seemed to flounder under the waves," he confirmed, shimmying down the mast.

Immediately they changed their pace and were no longer fighting the strengthening wind but turning with it and preparing for the storm. Mack smiled to himself, content that he'd read the situation accurately, for no ship of the line would have turned tail. In fact, this convinced him that had the ship been of the king's navy, they wouldn't have tried to stall them in the first place through false flags.

Mack glanced at Burke, who ordered the guns stowed and secured. He could see by the set furrow on Burke's brow that he thought Mackenzie had acted before thinking things through. Perhaps Burke imagined he'd put the crew and the ship in jeopardy.

"Why do I keep you around, old man?" Mack addressed his quartermaster. "You're nothing but a burr in my side."

"Better a burr in your side than a barnacle on your arse at the bottom of the ocean," Burke replied, the scowl softening with the banter.

Tiller reached the deck, and Mack called him over. "Well done, lad," he said. "A tot of rum. Spread the word, now."

Watching Tiller move away, the news of the stand-down ran through the crew faster than the water lapping the sides of the ship, and he smiled. At that unexpected moment, his thoughts drifted to the girl. Better she be off the ship as soon as possible. She was a distraction he couldn't afford when the stakes were this high.

Chapter Eleven

Maggs used to say curiosity killed the cat, and Flora felt she understood that more than ever. She immediately regretted sticking her head above decks. The choices were hopeless. Brace against the storm or return to the galley with its sour and fermenting smells. Thoughts of jumping overboard and calling an end to the struggle seemed a serious consideration. Would the storm never end?

And where was her mother now? Anger at the situation, being left alone combined with her inability to obtain any form of control, motivated Flora to rope up and attempt to be a seaman. She needed the air. The bowels of the ship were suffocating. The storm had raged so long, she wondered how much longer the creaking, leaking vessel could stay afloat. If she were to drown, she'd do so out in the open, not locked away. She inhaled deeply, the salt-sparked air offering a clean piece of heaven over the recesses of the ship.

When Flora had begun to retch, holding her stomach in a desperate effort to retain the contents, Dek, the cook clubbed her in the back with a wooden spoon. "Be gone with ye," he said, his Spanish accent pronounced. "Yur as green as a frog, and I won't have you befoul my kitchen."

The man, his bulbous nose a maze of broken blood vessels being the first thing Flora noticed as an object of concentration, had limpid, fog-filled eyes. The kindly turn of a face with cheeks seeming permanently heat-stained, creased at the corners. "You'll be fine," he continued as she stepped over the threshold toward the galley stair. "Go catch yur breath, then come back to get the grub ready for supper."

Barely able to nod, she fled up the stair, losing her footing several times as the *Navigator* tipped one way, then the other. Her wrist and knuckles ached where she continued to grip the meager railing while salt spray soaked her within moments. The cold coated her very bones, numbing her skin to the point where the tips of her fingers no longer tingled.

No stranger to cold and damp, having survived the streets of Halifax most of her life covered in rags she and her mother scrounged together, this was altogether different. Even Flora's teeth ached at the root with each breath.

At a loss of what to do or who to ask, her gaze sought the captain. Despite better intentions, he had become her compass. She suspected the same proved true for much of the crew, notwithstanding their drastic differences.

From the tall and wiry to the blunt-shouldered thugs and short stalky gunners and the ball boys not looking old enough to have left their mothers, let alone be on board a ship, each had the hardened stare of one who'd seen more of life than words could explain. While she may have considered herself tough, with her ability to survive street living, these steeled men provided pause for consideration. And not for the first time did she thank whoever was responsible for housing her with the more docile animals onboard. Burke, she thought. She feared, as she had never before been afraid, what would happen should any suspect her gender. Flora realized now she had acted on impulse, and that compulsion could be the death of her.

The captain had his back to her, and her shoulder burned where he'd touched her. Despite the momentary recognition, she understood he would do nothing to save her should the laborers suspect she was a woman. He'd warned her ahead of time and she'd paid him no heed. Now, he had what he wanted, the golden purse, and she was no more than disposable cargo.

Then, as she watched, Captain Mackenzie McGuire turned, and his piercing black eyes seemed to shoot straight through her. "Brace up!" His voice boomed above the milieu of the wind, rain, and ocean waves. "Tighten the rigging, you bastards, or we'll run to the lee!"

Even in the short time she'd been aboard, Flora knew running to the lee would mean the sails losing their strength, falling slack, and getting tangled in the ropes.

"Sure to create an opportunity to capsize," Tiller had said. "Neptune don't give no second chances. By the time a ship's managed to untangle the massive sails, all aboard could find themselves in the drink."

Just as Flora joined two others hauling on the leads, one of the cringles, the brass rings that held the corners of the sail where the rope ran through, started to tear. The rip resounded like thunder. Instinctively, she lunged for the foot, the bottom of the sail, amazed how much she'd picked up in such a short period of time. She needed to grab and repair it before the sail let go completely.

A large beefy man beside her caught her eye and grabbed the cringle. Her cap flew out to sea and her arms shook with the strain. Were her fingers mere matchsticks, she wondered, because they seemed about to break with the effort. Her shoulders strained with the effort to maintain her arms in their sockets.

The man, whose chest seemed as wide as she was tall, shouted for help. Within moments, two others with equally burly builds joined them.

Gathered in her flimsy grip, the sail, like a living thing, went from being taut in its harness of the wind, to flagging. Now the gale had all control. Clawlike, she gripped the cleat, but it bucked and jerked and lifted her into the air. She clung as the sheet whipped free of the confines of the ship's deck. The rope around her waist caught and held, jarring her spine. Flora kicked her feet, seeking purchase on something solid, but she flapped like an insect caught in a butterfly net.

Launched higher than the men could reach, aside from the uppermost cleats, all at once she realized she was the only thing holding the sail to the mast. Among the shouts, she twisted to search back over her shoulder. Much like her, only anchored to the deck, Tiller was the human cringle holding out against the squall's complete control of the ship.

The *Navigator* sank beneath the weight of the ocean before springing free. In horror, she flapped, waiting to be loosed of this fearsome grip, while they rode high into the air on the ridge of a wave. The white foam washed over her before they plunged again. Surely, within a few seconds, she'd be gone. Lost forever.

Then, in the next instant, the rope slackened. She

fell with the ship and banged against the rough oak planks. What little breath she'd been able to snatch into her lungs, gushed from her body. Blackness crowded the edge of vision as something tore and warmth trickled down her back. She wasn't lost, but she wasn't safe. Before thought could discern what had happened, the gale caught again, and Flora flew free to the air.

Billows cascaded. The rope tightened around her waist, and her arms would surely dislodge from their sockets. Hopeless, she lowered her head to stare back at the ship.

She watched the captain lunge from the quarterdeck.

"Hold her," he bellowed.

He had the rope in his grip. The others were tugging on the canvas.

"If we lose her, the ship goes too."

A mighty rip resounded, with its vibrations down the length of her arms. She could hold no longer. She'd been thrown clear. As she hurtled through space, the black mighty ocean waited to devour her. Time stalled as the gnarled gray waves, tipped with white, rose like teeth to claim their morsel.

Chapter Twelve

Mack grabbed the boom, adding his muscle to hold it in place. Tracking his gaze from the rope leading overboard, back to the top sail and then along the mast, he issued commands. Bloody hell, what had he been thinking, allowing that slip of a girl to try to pretend she'd be any match to the labor required of a grizzled seaman?

How long since she went over? Too long. He had hesitated, thinking they'd get canvas back in order. But of course, none but a few knew her sex. Her being new meant she was the most expendable of the crew.

Keeping count in his head, marking the seconds, he addressed the dual brawn of Malcolm and Barrett to fasten the cringle to a new cleat in the tarp before they lost the mast. Already the unnatural bend had caused a groan of the wood. They would have to repair any splinters of the thirty-foot timber with reinforcements.

Where was the girl? He'd lose her, rope or no, if he didn't act now. She wouldn't last long in the frigid water, besides.

Muttering curses and barking orders, Mack grabbed the only length of rope leading overboard. Unlike much of his crew, he could swim. Although he understood why many sailors couldn't, or more aptly put, chose not to learn, he had. Over the years, many had chided, wondering why anyone would want to prolong their impending death from the dark depth, but he'd always believed he had an obligation to save his own life, or at least prolong it for a while. Why expect someone else to risk what you were willing to save yourself?

With the cloth being furled to prevent further hazard, he threw off his hat and jacket. Soaked through, they landed with a thud. Then he grabbed Barrett by the scruff and pointed over the railing. "Pull me back."

"Oy?"

Mack could see nothing in the raging chop. No matter, the rope would lead him. Without further thought, he dove into the June water. He broke the surface, sputtered, and drew air while he could before a wave forced him under. He reached for and missed the lead. Already the *Navigator* was barely visible in the murk. He let the ocean take him down and made more progress underwater, his fist closing around the rope.

Squinting through the mist and salt, trying to blink the sting from his eyes, he scanned the surface for any sign of the girl. He yanked on the rope. Then suddenly a splotch of red showed like a beacon amongst all the gray. Arms flailing high, she fought to gain the surface.

She could swim. She faltered, but her movement indicated an ability, had the ocean not raged with such force.

One hand over the other, Mack inched his way to her, urging the stubborn wench to keep fighting.

Mack tried to shout, but his voice proved useless, drowned by the waves and wind. Though his progress labored slow, Flora's head kept ducking under the foam.

"Hold on, there, girl," he shouted uselessly. "Kick

your legs, goddamn you. Fight."

Then her head popped up again, and her gaze met his. Had he been close enough for her to hear?

"I'm coming."

Was that a smile? Impossible. Yet with the next wave, she flailed but remained above.

The chill of the water ate at his strength. The length of rope grew taut in both directions, and he glared back at his ship. There at the leeward both Barrett and Hemsley each pulled, and he was getting ever closer to his ship.

She was no more than ten feet away now, but that could have been fathoms, with the struggle it took to make any headway. He couldn't abandon his ship, crew, or the mission for a girl fool enough to trust him to stow her on board. It didn't matter she'd likely saved them all from capsizing by holding the ends together as long as she had. He couldn't create more risk now.

Then the reed of her voice trailed over the wind, rain, and madness of the ocean to reach him. "Captain!"

"Now or never," he told himself. With renewed might, Mack grabbed Flora's outstretched hands as a wave tossed her in the froth. Slipping under the same wave, Mack grabbed the slender wrist and held firm, pulling her limp body back to the surface. Wrapping the rope about his own body, cradling her close, urging whatever warmth he might have left to seep into her. He tugged twice and raised a large hand in the air, giving the signal to pull them in.

In a matter of moments, they were back on deck. Mack rolled to his knees, moving to remove the ice which would settle so quickly in the joints. Then he staggered to his feet and shook himself like a dog, the heavy curls of his too-long hair slapping him in the process. The men laid Flora's limp body flat. Shoeless, she didn't move. Coughing and sputtering, he forced air into his lungs past his scratchy swollen throat.

Taking a moment to ensure his ship had righted and they were in no immediate danger, Mackenzie stood above the scene and wondered if he'd been too late. She'd lost all color. Blue tinged the full purse of her lips and silhouetted her eye sockets in a skeletal fashion. Her shirt flapped open, revealing the strappings of her chest.

Upon reflection he questioned how any of them could have been fooled by her meager disguise. The delicate bones of her cheeks were prominent in the ivory of her skin. Her wrists, like a bird's, lay limp. He saw his thoughts reflected in a few of the crew standing nearby. He forestalled their query with a piercing glare.

Mack bent to retrieve his hat and noted the hint of gold through the clouds. The storm which had raged so long seemed willing to subside with the human sacrifice.

Ignoring the questioning, random, accusatory glances that seemed to wonder if he knew her gender and had participated in the ruse, he dismissed the men back to their posts.

"We've a ship to see to, men," he barked. "Burke. Divvy the repairs and see we remain on schedule. I want to weigh anchor by tomorrow on the tide."

"Aye."

"Goddamned shame," he muttered, bending next to the girl to close the rough seaman's shirt across her body and provide some dignity.

Without her quick movements to save the sail, the

Navigator would surely have been lost. Her sacrifice saved the rest. He retrieved his discarded coat and swung it around the slender form. She weighed little as he swung her up into his arms.

Hemsley appeared at his side.

"I'll take her below to have her prepared," he said.

"Aye, Capt'in," Hemsley said, removing his own cap. "What she done wasn't lost on the crew, and she deserves a proper burial."

Mack nodded, unable to speak, surprised at the lump in his throat.

Dek's cabin, the cook's abode, seemed too crass for a woman, regardless of low station. As he descended the steps, he changed course and rounded to his own cabin. He opened the door, and Duke's tail thumped against the floor boards. With a quick hand command, the dog remained at his own perch while Mack laid the limp form upon his bunk. Saddened, he swept the short hair back from her face. The pert, determined nose appeared more pink than as red as it had moments before.

Then she sneezed.

Duke barked once.

"Blessed virgin," he gasped and stepped back. Duke stood at his side, hackles raised.

A small lift of the lips greeted his response. "I've never been confused with the blessed one before."

Stunned, he grabbed her shoulders and lifted her away from the bunk, only to drop her again when her eyes fluttered open. A spasm of coughs wracked her thin frame. How had someone so delicate managed to hold the canvas in that wind?

Eyes now wide with the effort of expelling sea

water from her lungs, the green-gray gaze seemed unfocused, unaware of where she was. Overcoming his momentary confusion, he returned to her side and bent down.

He turned his attention only briefly to the dog to motion him back. Then he cupped her cheek, his thumb stroking the bone gently.

"There, lass," he said, tilting her so she lay more on her side than her back. "Spit it all up. You'll be better in a moment."

"Water," she croaked between gasps.

"Indeed." He reached for the pitcher next to his bunk. "Slow sips."

He didn't know what to do to minister to this slip of a girl, yet he couldn't bring himself to leave her alone while he fetched the cook. Mack had thought her lost. A swell of happiness threatened him, and he coughed to control its coming free.

Yet here she was alive, when he'd thought her dead and he too late to have saved her. A sudden protectiveness swamped him. With a nod, he determined to protect her as much as he could in these hostile waters until he could get her to safety.

"Thank ye," she said, her voice but a croaked whisper.

While bending close, he noted that her breathing seemed more normal, but tremors wracked her, coursing along her shoulders and down her arms. Where she'd been immobile only moments before, now every part of her seemed to vibrate.

"We must get you warm."

She nodded.

The blue-purple ring around her lips seemed even

more pronounced and dangerous now than when he'd thought her dead. His greatcoat, though damp, offered the best form of warmth available. He tucked the ends around her body, slightly amused at how it covered her from head to toe with plenty to spare.

"Something stronger, I think would do the trick," he mused, looking down at her shuddering body.

It was some time later before he could bring himself to leave her, assured she merely slept. He snapped his fingers and Duke joined him. By the time they gained the deck, the storm had abated, and the masts were secured. How close they had come to ruin, and not even in a battle.

"Burke?" He leapt to the quarterdeck, the big dog at his heel. "All secure?"

"Aye, aye, Capt'in."

Staring ahead to the dark and gloomy horizon, Mackenzie couldn't see anything. The rain continued to fall in sheets, but the worst of the storm had been left behind. Mind elsewhere, he felt for his spyglass, out of habit, only remembering too late it was lodged in his coat, which now covered Flora fast asleep on his bunk.

A woman in his cabin. Duke growled as though reading his mind. He couldn't speak for the Spaniard who captained the ship before him, but this was a first for Mack. Apparently the same proved true for Duke.

The thought made him want to chuckle. She had spunk, he'd concede, and at the moment he wanted nothing more than to spar with her as they had on the beach.

"You're in charge, Burke," he said. "I'm going to my cabin."

Taking the steep steps two at a time, hanging on to

the rails, Mackenzie made his way aft toward his cabin. It was a luxurious apartment. The Spaniard assuredly knew how to decorate, and Mack had delighted in his fine accommodations this last year. True, he'd gotten used to the arrangement. Larger than anything he'd had aboard other vessels and certainly more than those below, who had only their hammocks. The best, of course, had been in the trunk with the find of the missives and half of the golden map.

He hesitated outside the thick oakwood door, polished to a shine and fitted with a brass knocker and hinges. Should he knock? It struck him as absurd to announce his presence for his own cabin. A semblance of the feminine decorum remaining from his youth with his mother reasserted itself, and he rapped his knuckles against the wood in a sharp thud.

Hearing nothing, he entered.

There, still nestled within his bunk, lay the lady. The light from the porthole above haloed her fair hair, showing it a bright red in the limited light. To the side of the berth, a small table that served as his desk and meal area when he chose not to eat with his men sat with the tumbler of whiskey and a small meal.

The cook had been in, then.

Word would spread more rapidly than fire that the girl lived.

He strode to the trunk and pulled the key from its hiding spot, grateful he hadn't had it on him when he jumped in. Casting a glance at the serene face, he decided to chance changing his clothes. With his back to the bunk, he opened the trunk and gently moved the sketch of his mother to get to his spare clothes.

He stripped quickly and sponged the salt from his

body. As he bent to retrieve his breeches, Duke's low growl halted his movements.

"That's not a sight common to mine eyes." Her voice reached him as a traitorous flush consumed his skin.

Glancing back over his shoulder, he noted her propped up on one elbow, creamy shoulder exposed where his coat had fallen away.

Chapter Thirteen

It wasn't that Flora was unaccustomed to the sight of a man's body, but the sculpted perfection on this backside awoke something primal within the very center of her body. Her mother had used sex as a tool, forced to it as an occupation, a means of survival. Mother and daughter had never shared a conversation on coupling for mutual enjoyment, for surely, this strange sensation, though unfamiliar, promised pleasure. She'd never considered asking her mother about the relationship with Papa.

Flora regretted the words as they rolled from her tongue. She snagged the coat and hitched it high to cover her exposed body to her chin. She inhaled the scent of him left behind in the leather. One she remembered from waking on the docks when he'd saved her from Billy Seconds, that son of a bitch who was likely the cause of poor Maggs' death. The same that floated on the breeze on the beach before he agreed to take her on board. A slight intoxication made her eyes feel heavy, and she wanted nothing more than to curl back within the depths of this garment and live out her days. To have such a man as this be there to provide security translated into her version of heaven. The thought shocked her. She had thought she needed no one, but now she wondered—had she only survived this long to live in this moment?

In an instant of rushed rustle, the captain had grabbed his breeks and, with his lightly furred back ramrod straight, proceeded to dress. He turned to face her as he laced the front panel of his pants. His muscled chest sported an abundance of hair, which only seemed to increase her absurd awareness of his masculinity.

A quirked smile formed at the corner of his mouth. The scar appeared less livid and more a mark of his manhood—his courage. "I'm sure your eyes have seen so much more than a man's backside."

He bent to retrieve a fresh shirt. What magnificence to have a whole trunk of spare clothing.

She channeled her mother's easy banter to quell her nervousness. "I ain't never been aboard a ship afore," she said, helplessly watching his long fingers weave the buttons of his shirt into each hole. She shivered. Not from cold, as the cabin had a cozy feel. Someone had kept the stove in the corner stoked high while she'd slept. A dangerous thing to do in a storm. But the ship no longer rocked as it had.

All at once her mind traced back over the last hours of the storm. The ache in her shoulders, the tearing soreness in her upper arm, the dry parch of her mouth where she'd consumed enough sea water to drown from the inside out. Yet here she lay.

Then she'd heard his voice again over the tempest of the storm and the rage of the ocean intent on consuming her.

"I'm coming," he'd shouted, and she had heard.

If she could only stay afloat, he'd find her. He'd save her. She'd known this to the depths of her very soul. And he had.

But...Flora clutched the collar of the great

coat…now everyone knew the farce. He'd drop her at the first port. She'd failed in her end of their bargain.

"Take me with you," she whispered, traitorous tears swimming, altering all she saw. She cast her mind for a reason, any justification for why he should keep her on board. Now that the men knew of her gender, he'd drop her at the next port, wherever that might be. She offered no worth, no reason to retain her aboard. Again, she'd be alone and no better off than she was on the streets of Halifax.

"Please," she squeaked as he pulled on his boots. Fully clothed, he was imposing but didn't offer such a distraction as before.

He faced her now, hands on hips, dark brows looming like a plateau over his eyes.

She focused on his dark gaze, forcing herself not to look away. "If I can't work as the lads…" She shook her head, knowing that to be an impossibility now.

In his silence, she coughed, then shook her head. "I'll be your doxy." She nodded, warming to the idea and rolled up onto her knees on the bunk, keeping the coat hitched high. "Yes, that's it. Surely a life at sea is lonely. I could be yours."

He was on her before she was able to draw breath. His hands gripped her shoulders, and his eyes shone like coal afire. "No. That's not bloody it," he said, giving her a slight shake. "You're no bloody doxy. I knew that from the first when I saw you. A thief, yes. To be sure. I can almost smell the itch of your sticky fingers." He stared deeply into her eyes and nodded. "But you're no doxy, and I won't make you one."

The foolish tears which had threatened leaked free, clearing her vision.

"I can't go back," she said, raising her hands to stare at the palms. Would they always only be equipped for theft? In this moment, she prayed the opposite could be true.

Mackenzie released her and stepped back from the bunk. His breathing sounded almost as ragged as her own. "No, I can't take you with me."

Flora sniffed. "If you can't, who can?"

His jaw tightened. The muscle at the corner quivered. He raked fingers through the loose curls, and she realized this was the first she'd seen him without his queue. The hair did little to elevate his severe countenance. Instead, it made him appear more wild, dangerous. Flora felt an animal rush of her own, and as her hands trembled, she lowered the coat.

He stalled her with a look. The bark of his voice followed. "Don't."

"Why?"

He shook his head. "Don't," he repeated offering no further explanation.

"Where will I go?" She bit her lip, refusing further tears.

"I've broken the code, you see," he said, crossing to the door but making no move to leave. The dog's head moved as its gaze followed his path. "No women allowed on board. It would have been best for all had I left you to the sea."

Flora hung her head. Then she sniffed and straightened her spine. This would not defeat her. "But you brought me back, and I'll not go."

"I followed you because you saved the ship," he said, crossing the room to her in two strides. "But you'll go. I cannot control the natural impulse of all these men when it comes to their lusts. I might as well give up all order."

She shook her head. Words failed.

Mackenzie slammed his fist into the wall above her head. "God damn it." The words were coarse, barely audible in their sandpaper sound. "Don't you understand?"

He leaned in close to where Flora had refused to cower. His breath bathed her, and she wanted to inhale all of him—his strength—his sturdy presence—his courage. He didn't frighten her. She'd seen worse, far worse than he, in the gutters she had called home.

He looked at the flared fingers of his hand as they made a fist. "There isn't one among them that won't want a piece and think they deserve it simply because you came willingly on board," he continued. "It'll undermine me—do you understand that?"

He didn't shout, yet the words bounced and reverberated around the cabin as though he had.

"They won't go against ye," she managed at last, finding her voice. "I know they won't."

He laughed, a savage bite in it with no merriment. "How old did ye say ye are, lass?"

Flora tilted her chin. "How old do you need me to be?"

He slapped his fist to the bunk, reminding her of his universal rule, strength, and governance over her. "How old?"

"Twenty."

His nose flared. "Lie to me again and I will throw you overboard myself and turn my back on ye forever more."

She fought to hold his dark gaze, then lowered her

eyes. "Eighteen," she said, raising them again to meet his gaze. A spark flashed in his coal black eyes, and she added quickly, lifting her palm, "I swear."

A loud knock on the heavy door interrupted their standoff.

"Come," Mackenzie bellowed.

MacLeod of the red hair stepped gingerly inside the cabin. He met Flora's gaze briefly, then swung his attention to his captain.

"Burke sent me, sir," he began in a wheezy tenor. "Now that the storm's behind some, and we sees our way, Tiller spotted the ship again trailing us. Says she means business, that 'un."

"Bloody Judas," Mack swore. He straightened from her side and snapped his fingers so Duke came to his side. He scratched between the dog's ears. "That's no English frigate."

"Nay," MacLeod agreed. "Hemsley's assured they mean to board us."

"The hell they will." He turned back to Flora and lifted a fist, one finger pointing, his lips a harsh line, the line of vein intersecting his furrowed brow. "You'll stay put." Then he addressed his dog. "Duke. Stay. Guard."

She heard the growl in his tone and watched as the door shut and heard the bolt from the outside. The "Aye, Capt'in" in muted sarcastic tones rolled back in her intent, never to be realized, along with a host of other things she couldn't seem to say while he consumed all the air in the room.

Glaring once at the dog, Flora flopped back and let the coat fall from her body. How cold she'd been, and how close to death. She shivered, then shook the notion loose. "Keep moving on" had always been her and Maggs' motto.

She rolled and held her hand out to the dog. He surveyed her once, then approached, muzzle pushed against her palm. "Not so fierce, are ye?" She stroked his neck, and he leaned into her. "Not like yon master. Why bolt the door from the outside, eh?" She sighed and glanced around the cabin. "I've no wish to leave this luxury. Lock me in, says I."

She patted the dog on his rump and surveyed what remained of her garments. The strapping across her chest held. A lot of good that did her now. The thin cotton shirt hung in tatters, but the pants did better, though there wasn't much to them before.

She stood from the bed and braced against the heavy wood frame as nausea washed over her. Hot, then cold, traced across her skin, causing her to close her eyes and breathe deeply. Adjusting to the sway, gathering her balance, she stood unaided. "There now," she said, addressing the dog. "Only a moment and I've my sea legs back."

Then she giggled. "But where would they have gone? Washed overboard with me in the storm." She laughed out loud, happy to be alive despite what might come next.

Flora looked around again. The captain's desk lay cleared of paper, the ink blotter tidy, the ink stoppered with the quill close at hand, along with a sharpening knife. With tentative fingers she stroked the objects. She'd never had cause for the need of paper, though her mother had taught her how to read from scraps of the news in barrels left over from burning fires. She tested the drawers. They were locked. Not that she'd dare steal from such a man. She and Maggs always tried to pick easy marks—until the last.

A heavy weight descended on her heart. Maggs. She missed her mother's company above all else. The woman's twinkling laugh that lightened any mood. She could never feel without hope around her mother. Somehow even the worst situations were bright lights so long as Maggs' merry charm followed them. They might not have had an ideal life, but Maggs understood and accepted her daughter, protected her, and loved her. Flora couldn't imagine ever having that again.

"Small steps," her mother would say. "Just keep moving, my lovely."

Flora turned to the trunk. A man with so much would hardly miss what she would need. A shirt. Something fresh and clean. Oh, had she ever imagined such a thing? The trunk key remained in the bolt latch, and she understood at once that had he not been distracted by her catching him changing, it would likely have been bolted as tight as the drawers at his desk.

She flexed her fingers, glanced over her shoulder, and tiptoed to the door to put her ear to the latch and listen. She peeked through the keyhole. Nothing. Distant shouts, barely distinguishable, floated down the passage. That, along with what she now considered typical ship noise, eased her. No one was around.

Opening the lid, she glanced at the content. A drawing of a pretty woman lay to the side. "A wife? A sister? Mother?" Gently, she picked up the sketch and scrutinized the woman's face. The style of dress. The artist had captured a fire in the woman's eyes, and Flora determined, based on the dress and the resemblance of both nose and jaw, this was the captain's mother.

Careful not to crease the paper, she set the portrait to the side and rummaged through the clothing.

As she pulled a shirt free, a scrap of leather with writing fell to the floor. She bent to retrieve it and put it back in roughly the same spot when she noticed there were two pieces of leather. Of course. The golden purse. No longer was it a half map but a full and detailed description of...a treasure. And at the top of the second strip of material, in recent ink, was written, "Black's Gold."

Chapter Fourteen

Mackenzie lowered the spyglass. "All hands ahoy. Man the guns. Stand by the rigging," he ordered as he took up his stance next to Burke.

"Tiller's still aloft, sir," Burke said, the low tone of his voice carrying easily across the distance from wheel to rail.

"Good. We make for land. A spotter aloft's as necessary as cannon." Mack squinted in Tiller's direction, spotting the boy in the crow's nest. "Judas, I'd sooner balance walking a rope than brace the sway of that mast."

"Aye." Burke snorted and rolled his eyes. "Says he feels he's flying."

"Stupid lad. Flying." Mack huffed and turned his back as a small smile curved his lips. Certainly, Tiller's fearlessness at the height made his ship and crew stronger in times like these. "He'll be flying, all right, if we get hit by a rogue roll in this weather."

"He's tied," Hemsley said, coming to stand by Mack's side, drawing his own glass to his eye. "We're ready, sir."

Mack strode to the head of the quarterdeck. "Make ready then."

"All's ready," Hemsley yelled across to the men.

In unison, they answered. "Aye, aye."

"Steady on, lads." Mack lifted the spyglass again.

"I'm entrusting the *Navigator* to you, Burke."

"We're high in the water where yon beast ain't," the burly man responded, his tarred queue flipping against his neck. "We'll make for Cape La Have, around Moshers, and up the river a spell. If they give chase, they'll either fall on the shoals or sink 'er in the mud, for the area's a real bitch if you don't know it."

"More sail." Mack addressed Hemsley.

"Make haste, men," Hemsley bellowed above the fray. "All sails."

The ship keeled, bucked, and then caught the wind, the sails resounding like shot cannon as they drew taut with the effort of speed. They weaved first one way, then the other, while all the while the land grew closer.

A wake of white water trailed the ship, and soon the distance between them and their pursuer lengthened. An explosion sounded as one of the big guns of the enemy let loose.

Mack registered this with a sneer. "A wasted attempt, to be sure."

"Should we ask if they want us to stop and hold our arses in the air as well?" Hemsley called across the screech of the wind.

"The hell I will," Burke shouted back.

Mack laughed as the *Navigator* took the first turn around the island.

A few moments more and, on Burke's nod, Hemsley shouted, "Lower the mizzen. Less speed!"

"Perhaps she'll follow and sink in the mud, and we'll take her as prize," Hemsley quipped with a nod at Mackenzie.

"Perhaps," he replied. "But we've bigger bounty on our horizons."

"Aye, Capt'in, we do."

****

With the immediate danger behind them and unlikely to follow, and the weather more cooperative, Mack made to return to his cabin. The covert glances from his crew slowed his pace and reminded him he needed to be rid of the girl, and soon. His ship was no place for a budding beauty such as she. Mack cursed himself afresh for ever thinking he could trust the boyish disguise. Had the weather not been upon them from the onset, had Dek had the vision of other men, her identity would have been known far sooner than when she'd been tossed over.

On impulse, he bounded back up the stairs and checked Burke's maps. "As I thought."

"Aye?" Burke questioned.

"We'll reach our destination…when?" Mack glanced up at Burke, brows raised. "Within the day?"

"Confirming we've no pursuit, we'll anchor and make the island with the tide."

Mack nodded, closed the charts, and retraced his steps. Once anchored, he'd send one of the younger lads to take the girl to one of the larger nearaby settlements and see she be properly accommodated. Someone of her ingenuity would have no trouble making a place for herself. He'd provide some coin, and if all went as well as he hoped, perhaps he'd stop…

The thought died as it was born. "Bloody hell," he sputtered, entering his cabin. The open lid of his truck galvanized his attention before swinging to the girl swathed in his best shirt, sitting atop his bunk, smile broad. Her shapely legs poked out from beneath the hem where they crossed at the ankle. In each hand, she held the pieces of the map.

"Seems my passage is a very small price to pay for the bigger prize," Flora said, fluttering each half. "Shoulda looked closer. But then I had just lost me ma, been beaten up, and had nowhere to live."

Mack curbed the urge to lunge and grab the sheep's leather out of her grip. Instead, he turned and closed the door. After a moment's hesitation, he locked it as well.

"Looked like gibberish to me. Of no value at all when there's no coin to be had. But together, umm." Flora swung her legs over the side, swinging them like a child. "Maggs would 'ave been proud w' this haul, she would."

"You can read." Mack hadn't taken her for a simpleton, but the ability to read, in someone living on the street, did jolt his common assumptions. He'd known from the first she had quality. Still, he didn't like surprises, and had taught himself long ago never to assume. Yet here he was floundering with things outside of his control.

Her brows laddered toward the edge of her fiery red hair, and her green-blue eyes blazed. "Umm-hum." She laid one scrap of hide on each thigh and smoothed the contours. "Stupid name for a treasure island, though, is it no'?"

Mack took the two steps to his trunk, noting his mother's etching had been laid with care on top of his clothes, which remained neat and tidy. He mentally cursed himself for not having hidden the parchments with more care. He closed the lid gently and checked that the key remained in his pocket where he'd stowed it after changing, meaning to lock the cabinet before returning to his men.

He smothered a damn, and smiled at the girl. "That's the point, I think," he said. "If they called it Blackbeard's Island, well, that might give it away."

He watched as she stifled a giggle, then returned her gaze to the map. He had little doubt that he could grab the pieces without a struggle. Sure, he could easily overpower her, but Mack had no wish for violence with a woman of any kind and certainly not this one, who made his blood run hotter than any woman prior.

Her small frame sat rigid and expectant. This was a woman used to attack, and he had no intention of grappling with her. Housed in his cabin, amongst his men, on his ship, he could stand to be patient. At least until they weighed anchor.

The thought eased the immediate anxiety, though it allowed room for other notions. He needed to think. Every time he had a plan, she somehow managed to thwart it before it had gained purchase.

He needed to regain control of the situation. He crossed the cabin to settle into his desk chair, leaning back to settle his boots atop the secretary, crossing one over the other. The keys jangled together in his pocket, the sound a musical accompaniment to his apparent calm.

She didn't lift her gaze to him, yet he knew she followed his every move. His nerve endings tingled with this awareness.

"I thought the 'Black's Gold' name, just here…" She stabbed her pinky in the eastern section of the island map. "…might be you. But…" She paused, licked her full bottom lip, the tip of her pink tongue just skimming the surface before she shot him a look. "Why would you look for a treasure you'd buried?"

Mack nodded and folded his arms across his chest, cursing the erratic beat of his heart.

She tossed her gaze back to the maps and drew a corner of that full lip in between her teeth. The nibble awakened a desire in him to also taste the honey of those plump lips. Mack struggled not to change positions.

"But then I noted MDCXLVII," she continued, returning to study the artifact. "1647. That's a long time ago. What makes you think the treasure's still there?"

By the virgin, she knew her roman numerals as well. Mack shrugged, molding, with extreme effort, his features into placid composure. Shock roared in his mind. Reading was one thing, but understanding numbers and logic? Most of his crew could barely make their mark. How the hell had this girl been living on the streets, never mind trying to convince him she was a mere prostitute? Surely, at the very least, she should have been a lady's companion.

Her words tore him back to the present.

"You don't know the reputation of Tommy Two-Guns and his thugs. The likes of Billy Seconds, Tommy's long arm for those of us…makes no matter. You don't know 'im is all I mean," she said, raising her gaze to meet his. Her pale cheeks accentuated the purple smudges under her eyes. The smile gone, she placed one piece of ancient parchment gently over the other. "If that be he or his, following in that great ship, he'll no' give up. They think Maggs stole the map from Cain and killed 'im for it. But we got it from Billy Seconds…"

Flora lifted fingers splayed across her chin, and she tilted her head and pondered. "And we knew nothing of this." She gestured at the markings. "Which means—"

Mack sat up in his chair, and the wood creaked. "Cain took it from his father," he interjected, following her line of thought. "Perhaps in cahoots with Billy. Maybe they planned to take the old man down. Claim Halifax for their own. Even likely had a plan in place already with the ship. Too true, she's been on us since we left, and you can't do that overnight, assemble a crew and get 'er ready to journey. Then one or the other gets greedy, and Billy comes out on top, map in hand."

"Until Maggs."

Mack nodded, dropping his feet to the floor with an echoing thud and stood before her. "Until you."

"And you stopped him from finishing the job on the dock."

"That I did."

Her pallor had taken on a tissue transparency, and though she still sat on the bed, her large eyes looked glassy and she swayed a bit.

"Well, you were there." She lowered slender fingers to her still-bruised neck. "Wouldn't take much to connect when I'm no longer in Halifax. They'll know you've the whole map."

Mack's jaw tightened. "Tommy's not stupid." He crossed the room to drop back into the chair, elbows on his knees, letting his hand hang. "What makes you think Billy's still alive?"

Flora turned her head and raised her chin to indicate over her shoulder. "They've the ship, don't they? Doesn't matter whether Billy's alive or dead," she said sweeping her fringe back from her eyes. "Tommy's got the ship and the men, and he knows what you've got."

Why hadn't he considered that? He could have easily absconded with the map and not taken the lass.

"Devil be damned," he muttered, bracing a hand on each armrest. He'd suspected the ship of flying false flags. He'd even considered the banker behind the vessel. Still, he'd harbored the notion Tommy wouldn't know for sure he held the complete map and therefore would ease off once they lost them in the straits and narrows. Now, however…

Chapter Fifteen

Despite her earlier assertion to stay, Flora knew she should abandon the *Navigator*. Steal what she could from the cabin and jump at the next port. But she couldn't. She didn't think the captain would stop at any port now that they had figured out who followed. He wouldn't waste time.

Not that she'd developed qualms...but she'd seen too much. So much more appeared at stake than a quick stash and dash could satisfy. There was the Spanish copper next to the stone carving, and the small dagger at the bottom of his trunk that intrigued and made real what the map promised. Whatever the captain sought, she trusted it to be true, not some fairy tale. The map of a place called Oak Island, complete with riches, surpassed any kingdom on Earth. The mercenary in her, honed by Maggs all these years, couldn't leave with such a prize to be had.

"Better to have you disappeared, then found."

The cabin had been silent for so long, both lost in their contemplations. When at last he spoke, she jumped at the suddenness of the words. Did he mean to kill her? Her stomach tightened, and she glanced around for a weapon.

"Nay, lass," he said, rising to his feet. "I wouldn't have jumped into the drink to gather ye back had I wanted ye dead. I'd not have wasted the energy."

She was no longer surprised at his ability to read her thoughts. Placidly, Flora handed him the map, having committed the contents to memory. Even now, she could close her eyes and visualize the smallest details, like the narrow peninsula linking the island to the mainland, or the distinctive oak tree marking the location, which she assumed offered the origins of the name. That was part of what had made her a good thief and able to get away. She'd always been able to memorize at a glance any street maps and details others seemed to miss.

He nodded at her, and his face rearranged into a suggestion of settling to a decision. "For the remainder of your stay, you'll stay here…alone." He'd gained his feet and now paced one way, then the other, covering the space in only a few strides. His black eyes glittered. "Won't be long. We'll be land bound by tomorrow's tide."

More than she expected.

"Is that clear?"

"Y-yes," she stammered and swallowed down the lump in her throat. "But what happens once we're there?"

He shook his head and brushed lint from the elbow of his jacket. "I'll work that out later," he said and returned to his trunk. After a moment he stood and tossed her an aged pair of trousers. "Now, come along."

"Where?" Flora couldn't move from the bunk. Sudden fear gripped her like a steel cage. Tickling needles assaulted the backs of her knees, leaving her immobile.

"No questions, lass." His eyes moved to the clothing, and he lifted his chin. More than a day's stubble darkened his olive skin. "Now. Before the men start to wonder if they'll have a turn with ye."

Flora controlled the loosening grip of her bowels with effort. She jumped to her feet, pulled on the breeks, almost tipping over with her shaking limbs, trying to regain her balance. Hoisting the pants high, she tucked in the shirt ends and tied the string of the britches. Being barefooted didn't bother her. Most of the crew labored without footwear. However, being bareheaded left her feeling exposed.

The captain seemed to sense her thoughts and quickly returned to the chest for a rag. He didn't need to elaborate. She tied the ends swiftly and managed a smile as they stepped across the threshold.

As they reached the upper deck, Mack gripped her upper arm, though the pressure wasn't painful, and proceeded, holding her before him.

"Gather 'bout, men," Mackenzie called, and the crew immediately obeyed.

"We have been played the fool by this wench." Mack shook Flora, and she allowed her body to slacken, pliant, like a rag doll, understanding immediately his intention. "She boarded our ship willingly in the disguise of a boy."

Muttered curses and general howls sailed across to her. The captain silenced this with a look across the sea of faces.

"I'd say she be a danger and a disturbance, like all women." Mack glared around at his crew.

"Curse a female on board a ship," a seaman shouted, heard above the hum of others.

"Aye," Mack agreed, nodding. A long moment passed, in which Flora forgot how to breath. Then his voice, strong and vibrant, cut across the air and demanded to be heard. "But not this lass."

Flora turned her head so quickly she heard the snap of her neck.

"This 'un…" He shook her gently again and pushed her farther within the gathering crowd of haggard men.

Flora prayed he wouldn't let go. How had she not noticed before how dangerous they all appeared? How had she not noticed the predatory hunger in their eyes? Or the cutthroat pirate nature of the captain himself. Sweet Judas priest, she couldn't stay on board without protection.

His chuckle made her heart stop. "She be our good-luck charm," he continued, and she thought she would faint with the strain of not knowing what would come next.

Mixed murmurs and confused expressions surrounded Flora, who felt as out of her depth and baffled as the throng.

"Without this lass, we'd all be having dinner with Davey Jones this night," he bellowed. "Without this 'un here, we wouldn't be on our way to collecting the biggest treasure hoard this side of the Atlantic."

Flora gazed around, amazed. She figured all the men knew already. Now, she puzzled it together. The shrewd captain gave little up until he had to.

"Nay, lads, we keep 'er and treat her well until that mangey-bearded Eddy Teach's gold fills our hold and weighs us so low in the water we may need to pull the ol' *Navigator* to tide by hand."

With the astounded whispers came a resounding whoop. Fists curled and pounded the air now thick with excitement.

"What say ye, lads? This lass be our charm, men," Mack roared into the fray. "Pure luck. Heed me, now."

The men fell silent with the command.

"Hear me well," he said into the hush. The low, vibrating tones of his voice carried without effort. "Any man found within even a few feet of this wench will find his balls cut off before he can utter an excuse."

The words were uttered with a dispassionate carelessness, and Flora didn't doubt neither she nor any of the crew questioned that he meant every word.

"Return to your posts. There be work to be done, plans to be made. Treasure awaits, lads," he said with a smile which animated his face as she hadn't seen before. "Treasure the likes we could never have imagined possible. We be after the legendary Black's Gold."

"You heard the captain," Hemsley shouted as Mack pushed Flora before him to retrace their steps. "Back to work."

As they entered the cabin and Mackenzie released his grip, Flora turned and laid him a punch. The small bones of her hands seemed to shatter as they deflected off his square jaw, doing her more damage than him. Backing away holding her hand to her chest, she screamed, both relieved and angered, "Who the hell do you think you are? You've no right…"

"I've every right," Mack said slowly and clearly, not showing any signs that she had struck him. He closed the distance. "You chose to board my ship under—"

"In exchange for the map." She flung an arm toward his now-locked trunk.

"So you have granted me every right that I may take," he continued, as though she hadn't spoken. His voice dropped, and he looked down at her, his smoldering gaze raking her face. "In fact, you offered me more than I asked."

"You'll not have me." She spat, uncertain where that had come from, since he'd made no move toward her. Yet he indicated his crew would make such assumptions.

At this, the captain laughed. The chimes of his mirth echoed off the cabin walls. "Oh, my dear," he said, trailing a finger along the length of her arm before moving to take his seat at the desk. "'Tis you who tried to convince me you were a doxy. May I remind you, I've no interest in the likes."

Flora hung her head, uncertain. For the first time in her life, and without Maggs, she didn't know what to do—had no purpose. "I'm not."

He glanced across at her, his hard, black glaze seeming to soften just a bit. "I know, lass."

He rose then and crossed the room to stand looking down at her. He rested his fingers gently on her shoulders. "Make no mistake, though," he said, his voice almost a caress, and she felt the tingle behind her knees, this time not unwelcomed. "If I want you, I'll take you."

His unique scent of salt, spice, and hard work wafted over her. Flora tilted her head back to look at him. She opened and closed her mouth, fighting to regain her normal quick-witted retorts. Reason had fled within his close proximity. No words emerged.

He dropped his hands and strode for the door. Pausing at the entrance, he cast her a look over his shoulder. "I've more pressing duties than to claim a maidenhead."

Then he turned on his heel and left, locking the door behind him.

Chapter Sixteen

The image of moist parted lips and large doe eyes staring up at him from pale, vulnerable features made his steps stagger as he moved toward the upper deck. How could he expect his men to behave around someone who so easily tightened his own loins? That was how women cursed ships.

"God damn it," he muttered, taking the steps two at a time. He had no need of such distractions. He couldn't stop now and risk that bastard Two-Guns catching up with him. Not when he was this close. So he was stuck.

Her words stung even though he'd given her no cause. Mackenzie had never known a woman so brazen. The urge to kiss that impudence away had swamped him to the point where he'd had to flee his own cabin. Better to leave her be, for the moment. They'd make landfall within the day. Between now and then, he prayed a solution would present itself.

For now, there could be no doubt they would run up against the enemy in search of the same prize. Any notion of sending the woman on her way was shelved. Dumping her would only leave them vulnerable at this stage. The banker might know where they were bound, but that cunning Pirate Blackbeard had set many a trap, and without the map to guide them through the pitfalls, they might as well be floundering in the ocean during a storm.

As the moon rose over the horizon, a plethora of stars in its wake, the islands they had been navigating all day to avoid open water turned to shadows. The silhouette ahead served only to heighten the island's resemblance to a leaf. From their angle of approach, the stem, clearly visible, highlighted the rounding bottom which hid the narrow eastern section.

Mackenzie pulled a piece of the map from his pocket. He'd long ago deciphered the code—the key to the many mysteries and hidden passages of this treasure trove. Without the proper decryption for landing, tunnels, and booby-trap avoidance, one might as well be like a gopher and start digging holes which would never amount to anything.

He drew out his spyglass and surveyed what he could in the fading light. The full lunar light hardly helped at this distance. He pointed, his arm echoing the angle of the glass. "We'll land just there."

"Potential ambush?" Hemsley questioned, his own glass raised to his eye.

Mack shook his head. "Peninsula's fairly narrow. No trees. Hard to hide," he said and whistled. Duke came bounding. "We'll be cautious. I'll go in the longboat and take the dog."

They'd done this many times before, and no one proved better than his four-legged companion for spotting trouble.

"Right-o."

"With any luck at all, we'll have what we need within the day—we can risk no more and still get away." He slapped the ends of the glass together and laid it back to rest in its inner pouch in his greatcoat. "Any longer than that, we'll attract too much attention."

"Looks peaceful enough," Burke commented, commanding the crew to reduce sail and drop anchor. "'Course, they always do."

"Aye, they do," Mack agreed, mentally checking he had everything he needed for the swift trip to the beach. Gun. Knife. Maps. Dog. "I'm counting you did your job and lost those bleeding bastards."

Burke grunted.

Mackenzie adjusted his cap, turned to his two most trusted men, and tipped two fingers off the brim. "Oak Island be ours for the taking."

"Aye, Capt'in. She is that."

Mack grinned and launched himself over the rail and into the small cutter already manned with two seamen armed and ready. He caught Duke as he bounded behind him, then allowed the boat to be lowered to the side of the *Navigator* and into the sea. Picking up a set of oars, they stroked against the current and to the shore.

He learned, since the opportunity presented itself, that the island had been so named for its once abundant oak groves. Mackenzie could see despite the darkness that the farmers, being so close to the mainland, had done away with many of the native trees in order to plant their crops. No one lived on the small scrap of land, but who could blame them for putting it to good use in feeding their families.

For the first time since obtaining the first half of the map, Mack allowed himself to envision what life might look like after the cache was unearthed. He wanted to quell the excitement, but an easy imagining of a life with a family of his own sprang forth. A wife with flaming red hair and hidden riches of her own.

Duke growled softly, pulling him back to the task at hand. He paused the rowing to stroke the dog's ears. No hackles. Just alert. "Good boy."

Rumors had abounded for decades since the demise of Blackbeard, rumors of what his hidden trove might amount to, but none had known where to look, even as a starting point, and even fewer dared to imagine. Everything from the king's own treasure, stolen out from under the very eyes of the French by the fleeing English when they lost their fortress on Cape Breton, to the chalice Jesus used during the Last Supper, supposed to have been found somewhere on the Mediterranean coast, had been reputed to be buried.

Mackenzie wasn't quite sure what to expect, and until now hadn't wasted much time on the contemplation. Anything was something.

"We're about, sir," called one of the seamen in low tones.

Mackenzie nodded. Gravel struck the bottom of the boat. "Guns cocked, gentlemen, if you please."

"Aye," the two hummed in chorus.

"One remains, oars at the ready." He pointed aft. "You. With me." He leaped from the boat. Water lapped the top of his boots; rivulets of cold water trickled down his calves. The buzz of frenzy burned his nerve endings, and he was grateful for the chill. Mack snapped his fingers twice and Duke jumped out of the boat and splashed to his side, tail pointed, muzzle alert.

Careful steps brought them to the pebbled beach. Hardly any trees presented themselves for ambush. Still, he snapped his fingers twice and pointed. The dog took off and ran along the edge of the tall grass, then returned, tail wagging.

"Good lad." Mack patted the dog's head and scratched his ears. "Well done."

"Moon be bright, Capt'in."

"Aye, 'tis that, lads," Mack agreed, not bothering to conceal the broad grin. "'Tis a fine enough night for us to be about our business."

Chapter Seventeen

With the code broken, the map presented as clear as a fine summer day. Mack planned carefully with both Burke and Hemsley. Hesitating only a moment, he had Flora accompany the ground party ashore. Better she be under his watchful eye than alone with stags anxious for the thrill of treasure.

In addition to the girl, a crew of ten men accompanied them, leaving a solid contingent—less the distraction of a woman, in charge of the ship's keep.

Once off the peninsula, the map allocated the broad end of the sou'west portion of the "leaf" into degrees. Easy to follow for a mariner used to such things to navigate. So much harder for any landlubber who may have inadvertently come into ownership of the directions. Mack considered the banker with a sneer. By his estimation, the only contact Tommy Two-Guns had with the ocean were the ships he either owned or stole from their owners, once docked.

Mack consulted the directions while the others assembled the tools, hefting equipment onto their backs and onto gurneys carried by two-man teams. Trudging over the uneven beach, they were to make their way to the ninety-degree point of the curve. Mack was sure Eddy Teach, better known more famously as Blackbeard, had designed this specifically, in his notoriously traitorous brain, to make the going more difficult for those uneducated, non-seafaring fools who would seek *his* fortune. Mack harbored no illusions. The two etchings, as cryptic as they were, hadn't been designed to give the treasure away to others, but to allow Eddy to find it at will should his memory lapse in his old age.

Fellow thieves, pirates, or treasure hunters would have to understand mathematics, tides, and seasonal discrepancies common to the ocean to pull off the heist. Fortunately for Mackenzie, what he didn't know he was convinced the skill sets of his handpicked men like Burke and Hemsley would supply.

Placing men strategically around the beach to mark these spots with stones etched quickly with reference numbers, he charted the area with footfalls, finding the ninety-degree point in moments. From there, they aligned to the stars to chart a direct path through the clearing, which would take them to the stone's cross. Six stones coordinated according to the stars. Polaris with the top stone and on through the Plough to Dubhe at the midsection and Merak for the southern locator.

"This is our night, boys," he said, and found Flora's gaze in the gloom. Her luminous eyes locked with his in the excitement, and he knew in that moment he could take her quick and hungrily. Perhaps he should have left her onboard. He shook his head. Now that he had been saddled with her, he wanted her with him and left for later the questioning of why.

With effort, he dropped from her gaze and turned to the men. "Now step lively. I want to take best advantage of the shroud of darkness."

They covered the ground quickly. Mack considered the stone might be hard to spot and kept scanning the rough terrain for signs while Burke navigated celestially. Once aligned, they stopped and searched.

"Here," Flora said, standing atop a boulder. "'Tis marked." She jumped down and ran her palm along the engraving.

"I'll be damned," Hemsley said. "She do be our good-luck charm. Well done, lass."

Mack strode across the clearing and touched her shoulder. A current of excitement flowed from her, raising the hairs along his bare forearm. "Well done, indeed."

He bent to peer at the symbols.

"They be just like the code on thy map," she whispered softly into his ear.

No one could possibly have heard, and he didn't chance the tenor of his own low tones to travel, so he turned to look at her and nod. Having cracked the cypher, he could read the rock easily. The stones were exactly where they were supposed to be, and Mack had to swallow down a laugh of pure elation.

He stood and found Burke at his side. "Polaris."

"Aye, she be true north."

Mack laid the two pieces of leather atop the concave surface of the boulder. He touched Flora's hand. "Fetch me the lamp, lass."

From Dubhe, they would turn ninety degrees for the western end of the cross. One hundred paces would mark where the next rock should align. At this angle, if they dug straight down for two meters, they would come across flat shale stones, under which they would find the key to the entrance of the shaft. That shaft would carry them across the middle of the island to the actual entrance to the treasure's hiding place. The shaft's entrance, however, was located under the eastern boulder, equal distance in the opposite direction from the key.

Without the correct entrance coordinates, any other access would fail, for as soon as the tide came up, the shafts would fill with water funneled in through the beach according to the waterways laid by the shale stones.

He patted Flora's hand. "Go ye now with Burke and find the entrance for us, lass."

Burke nodded, repositioned his sextant, and started pacing out the next quadrant while Hemsley directed the crew where to dig.

Mack shook his head. He had to hand it to Blackbeard. Even at this early stage, he could appreciate the magnificence of such a constructed scheme. The design ensured whoever sought the treasure would be lost without the details of not just the map but the decoded cypher, which then allowed one to read the engravings on each of the boulders. While the seamen dug, Mack backtracked to each of the stones and carefully reproduced the engravings on the back of one of the pieces of leather, taking care to recreate the code exactly as it appeared on each rock. He focused extra attention on rendering the worn areas eroded by time and exposure to the elements. He had a feeling the messages would prove useful later.

"Capt'in," Tiller called ahead of coming into view where Mack knelt by the southernmost rock.

"Aye," he called, standing as his heart doubled its beats when he saw the boy running with an object clutched to his chest.

Tiller handed over what initially looked like a

stone. But his fingers immediately felt what his eyes didn't see. Did Blackbeard himself take the pains to complete all of these engravings? Surely not. Mack shook his head. Yet…based on the legend of the bloody bastard, he would have trusted no one else. Still, Mack raised the lantern and held the stonework closer to inspect.

The outline atop featured a tricorn hat with the fox—Blackbeard's personal symbol—poking his head out at the left. Within the hat, the unmistakable crest of the *Nuestra Senora de Atocha*, his famous ship, which sank in 1622.

"Devil be damned." He raised a hand to his brow to swipe the sweat aside.

He turned the masonry over, weighing it slightly, balancing it in his palm. "She be a fine bit of paperweight," he said to Tiller, whose already bulbous eyes seemed to swim in the plainness of his face.

The boy croaked in response and pointed at the series of pin-like protrusions reaching toward the sky from his outstretched hand.

""'Tis it, then," he said, seeing the remainder of the crew now assembled with Hemsley, waiting a few feet off.

Within moments they had reached Burke and Flora. She knelt by the boulder, her fingers playing across the symbols. "Thirty feet, twenty-degree angle," she said, standing. "Miss it and, I suspect, we'll miss the entrance entirely."

In that moment, audience be damned, he could have taken her in his arms and kissed her blind. No one but the two of them understood the code. "Must we move the stone to begin?"

"Aye, we do, Capt'in," Burke confirmed. "The angle and depth depend on where we start, according to the lass."

Mack knelt to transcribe the code with the others on the back of the second cloth. "How much time till dawn?"

"Four, maybe five hours," Hemsley said.

"Tiller…" Mack turned to the lad. "Return to the *Navigator*. The crew needs to shelter the ship on the next tide. On my command, they are to be alert, man the guns, and you take the watch. Take MacLeod with you. He stays on the beach. Any approach by land or sea. You understand."

"Aye. Aye."

"Away with you then." He watched the two boys disappear into the overgrowth before he turned to the remainder, who shuffled from foot to foot in anticipation of starting. "We begin."

Chapter Eighteen

To Flora, the night passed quickly. Too quickly. She bit the skin along her thumbnail until the pain of raw flesh halted the gnawing. Never in her life had she been treated as an equal. Yet the captain not only consulted her on the translation but seemed to trust her interpretation without further question. Though she'd given him no reason to do so, to even trust her at all, still he did. She knew this instinctively.

A frisson of excitement shot down her spine as she thought of the heavy-browed, black-eyed man. Her heart grew and swelled each time he looked at her, elation and anticipation evident in every crease and sun-baked crag of his face. It was as though she were viewing him for the first time. The boy he may have been. The adventurer who took to the sea.

This night had opened a friendship, as though he were allowing himself to be seen. Giving her permission to participate in his joy.

As the sun crept above the horizon, Burke triangulated the angle and the depth of the shaft before them, keeping them on pace. They pondered the stone trenches revealed at the bottom of their dig. Only a small body, while the tide was down, would be able to traverse the trench to the next phase as outlined by the map. If they were going to reach the treasure, this was the moment. It was obvious the water level here rose and fell with the tides, with some sort of underground connection to the sea.

Seeming to anticipate her thoughts, Mackenzie shook his head. "It's too dangerous for a girl," he said. "The tunnel could collapse. This place is ancient, and there's no telling what critters have done to the stabilizers, if indeed there are any support braces still intact."

"Tiller, then," Burke offered.

Hemsley dropped into the trench and shone the lamp. He shook his acorn-shaped head. "Narrows as she goes down."

"Then we send for one of the boys on board." Burke pointed back to the far side of the island.

"We wait, and we lose the tide and risk discovery," she said, hands on hips. "You either want this or not. The locals will know you've been—may even know now."

Flora watched the captain shake his head and then grudgingly nod.

"The boys are too young, too inexperienced, and she's right. It's only a matter of time before Tommy Two-Guns' men find us." The captain paced back and forth, finally lifting his head to the moon. "Our destination was no secret, and we've less than three hours at best 'til daybreak."

Flora tightened the scarf around her head and wrapped rags over her hands.

Mack consulted the map. "Shimmy through this trench until you reach the opening. There's another entrance. I know it," he said. "There's nothing to help if the tunnel collapses."

Flora swallowed and blinked several times before

she could answer. "Aye."

"High tide's a-comin'," Burke said.

"Then I'd better be off."

Striding to her side so the other men would not be privy to their conversation, Mackenzie took her by the shoulders. "You've a share in the profit," he said simply. "You came aboard for the chance of a better life, and by Gawd you'll have it."

Her head wobbled, and she gave up on speech. With a final nod, she jumped into the hole. She was their lucky charm, and she'd see this to the end.

Feeling the spirit of Maggs with her, she gathered her strength of courage and, holding the lantern ahead, wiggled her way into the first few feet. Quickly the damp gathered and her knees and elbows became coated with mud. At first the murmur of the men accompanied her, but now, only the pulse of the Earth sounded. Ocean lapped and thudded all around, making her feel as though she were swimming through the depths. Unlike when she'd been tossed overboard, she wasn't afraid but intrigued.

How had Blackbeard devised such a place? According to legend, he killed just to keep himself sharp. Had he really killed the crew who labored to house his lifetime of treasure? Trust no one and no one can betray you.

The farther she progressed, the more she felt as though she were in Mother Nature's womb. The thought offered such comfort she momentarily lost any fear of going into the bowels of this island which could collapse on her at any given moment.

Inches and eternity kept pace until she could faintly detect a whoosh of air—that battered the flame of the lantern. Casting a glance behind, all was black as pitch. Sudden claustrophobia gripped her. But she couldn't go back. The men were depending on her—he had put his trust in her.

Then her hand holding the lantern fell down a hole, and she screamed. The light slammed against the rock face, and the fragile flame sputtered.

Mack's voice echoed down the passage. "Are you there? Has there been a cave-in?"

Gulping air, heart hammering through her ribs, she shook her head, then realized he couldn't see her. She rounded her chin to her shoulder, barely able to move in the tight space built for a worm. "I think I've reached the trench."

"Good girl."

Wiggling forward until her head came free of the trench, she lifted the light. Pushing to free her other arm, she crept forward. How deep? Surely, she'd kill herself in the fall from this hole.

She glanced around the open cavern and started to laugh. The sound wedged into the space with her and bounced off the walls. The small flame seemed to grow in both intensity and size. Golden light radiated on a sight of fortune she could not possibly have dreamed.

She turned her body so her back faced the floor and jerked and squirmed until the trench loosened its grip on her body. With a small thud, she landed on the splintered surface. The earth shifted and the walls thundered. Mud and rocks showered upon her head.

She stood on shaky legs. "Say what you will," she muttered, standing to look around. "Brilliant."

No matter how someone went about it, from the shaft above or from the trench, there were so many ways to go wrong. Two large chests and a scattering of open treasure were positioned rather perilously on two wide planks set into the walls. Disinclined to move farther, Flora viewed the open pieces as the trap they were. Moving any of it, especially the chest, would alter the weight distribution and the soil. This in turn would shatter the only posts holding the ceiling and cause the shaft above to cave in. Then the chest and all it contained would be lost.

Genius.

Flora reached behind for a handful of dirt. She dropped the discarded soil down the empty space below her feet and waited to listen to it fall. In seconds the rebounding noise came back to her.

Water.

Was there a possibility of the captain positioning the *Navigator* to gather the treasure by sea?

She needed to return to him. Tell him. Reaching with both hands, Flora gently opened the closest chest. It moved on the planking, and the earth shook. She steeled herself and proceeded more carefully.

The chest was filled to maximum capacity. She could feel jewels and paper.

"Paper," she said aloud to herself. "What good is paper?"

Forgetting momentarily about the time factor, Flora wrenched the piece of paper loose and held it up to the lantern to read in the dim light.

"By his majesty's coat of arms, I give thee the right to any land for which you are able to take by barter, trade or force." This meant nothing to her.

She reached back in. Gold tinkled. Bullion. She pulled it free of the oversized trunk and scrutinized the insignia, then placed it in her pocket. By her own eyes, the king's own bullion.

Of a sudden, Flora heard the yelling through the tunnel. "'Urry, girl! 'Urry! The tide's a-coming!"

The words sent a shiver of panic through to her very bones. Rushing, she scrambled back into the trench, the tinkling of the trinkets marking her pace.

She was feet in when the blackness consumed her. The lantern remained on the planks where she'd forgotten it. Though she knew there was only one way, breath seemed to flee from her body. Sweaty and struggling to hold back her screams, at last she felt the wet of the cold sea and open air. She froze, disoriented. Then she heard the captain's voice.

"Come on, girl!" He sounded like he was just ahead through the black. "The tide's coming up quickly."

"I can't see."

"I'm here." His voice cushioned, added strength to her tired limbs as she inched forward as quickly as the small space allowed.

Chapter Nineteen

Mack threw his hat to the ground and only just refrained from stamping it to bits in his frustration. "God damn it," he muttered under his breath. The stars had flitted back to their daytime hiding place, the moon had set, and the sky was making its transformation from ink to indigo quickly. His breath hissed through his clenched teeth while he fisted and unfisted the coins and gems Flora had given him. "We've no choice but to go back and bring the ship around and try at the next tide."

Reluctantly, he pointed to the drawing Flora had made that morning. He was not in the mood to admire the brilliance of Edward Teach in protecting his treasure through this elaborate maze of trenches and traps. He'd given Blackbeard's maps much consideration and planning before he, Burke, and Hemsley set their sights on Oak Island. They'd prepared, or so he thought, but time was against them. The banker, or if not he, then his thugs, Mack was sure, would soon be upon them.

Mack regarded the foam of sea water sloshing down the recently evacuated tunnel. Had Flora not come back when she did, she surely would have drowned, with no way to escape. He looked toward the small cluster of men, and his heart inadvertently skipped when he spotted her small shivering form standing off to the side.

He pointed two fingers at her. "That's twice."

She met his gaze, eyes wide, arms hugging around her slender frame. But she didn't shrink back. He couldn't help but admire her fortitude.

Bending to retrieve his hat, Mack flapped it against his pant leg. Then he regarded each of the assembled men. He held up his palm, revealing the small sample of treasure.

He allowed a small grin, then bared his teeth. "This treasure be ourns," he shouted, closing his fingers around the gems again and holding his hand high in the air. "Did I not say she be lucky?"

"Aye."

Amongst the shouts of ascent, he regarded Flora's smiling face, and his body reacted. "Did I not say?"

"Aye, Capt'in."

He'd have to put her ashore soon. She'd become a temptation he might not be able to resist much longer. In twelve hours, with the loot onboard, he'd find somewhere safe, set her up like the lady she deserved to be…and then be on his way.

Why the hesitation? He knew the answer and buried it deep.

Back aboard the *Navigator*, having left a small group to guard the entrance from land, he marched to the helm. "Haul anchor and raise the masts," Mack bellowed. "Time's a-wastin'."

He logged the coordinates and left Burke to the maneuvers. Being light in the haul would mean they could pull closer to shore.

Flora had given him a detailed description of the cave. He'd have to get inside via the sea. They couldn't widen the trench—that could cause the walls to collapse. There was no telling how deep the water below, or how strong the currents.

No, he'd have to gain entrance from the ocean, and from there, he could assess how to extract the chests. He lowered the glass and retrieved the paper Flora had provided away from the men.

He expected gold and gems, but this… He knew the emblem. Every sailor from the time they were pressed into service knew the king's crest. He fingered the rich, thick paper, still glossy despite the age.

"By his majesty's coat of arms, I give thee the right to any land for which you are able to take by barter, trade or force."

Did this mean anything to him and his crew? Could he use it the same way the infamous Edward Teach had? Eddie, who had been sanctioned by King George I. The same king who had decreed that any pirate who surrendered to a British governor by September 1718 would be pardoned for all piracies committed and could even keep his plunder. Blackbeard and his ship, the *Queen Anne's Revenge*, and his three hundred men had plundered and been allowed to take at his whim by the king's own authority.

Mack doubted their own good King William IV would acquiesce similarly.

Striding to the rail, he pulled the spyglass from his breast pocket. Dawn spread like a purple bruise on the eastern horizon. "Damnation." He needed to be on his way. He wasn't known for sharing. His crew had never been afraid of earning their keep, hence their portion. He had no intention of splitting his men's portion or fighting over the treasure with the likes of those

Haligonian thugs who didn't belong on his ocean.

To make matters worse, if he dallied too long, those damned British would be upon them. The longer he dallied, the closer they came to the hangman's noose.

"Oi, Capt'in," Burke called, breaking through Mack's reverie. "I can bring us in real close now, but come low tide…"

As Burke let the question hang, Mack scrutinized the cliff face. The perception from the sea varied drastically from the land. He should have known better. Here the rocks shot thirty or more feet above the crashing waves, with no sign of the cave entrance. From their vantage point at the trench, he'd imagined the cave would be accessible in the high tide and they wouldn't have to wait so long.

"Bloody hell."

"Young Red swims like a fish," Hemsley said, sidling up to his side.

"Not alone."

"You go."

Mack smiled and nodded, already planning.

"Only person I know swims better than Red is you."

"Only 'cause the rest of you refuse to learn."

"No need." Burke smiled. "When it's time, it's time. No need to prolong the agony."

"And you think knowing how to swim would prolong the agony? What about holding out until someone can get to you?"

Burke laughed outright and slapped Mack on the back. "We're not all as lucky as you and the girl," he said. "Two peas in a pod, they say. Both like cats."

"Cats?"
"You've nine lives."

Chapter Twenty

Flora shot up out of the bunk with the thump of feet across the threshold. "Christ almighty. You scared the living life outa me."

She hadn't known such exhaustion. Once she'd scrubbed off the mud and grime as best she could, she tossed her clothes in a heap in the corner. Aside from the shirt she lifted from Mack's locker at the foot of the bunk, she lay naked.

Her intention had been to clean her meager rags prior to his return, but the temptation of the berth and a moment to rest her head was too much to resist. And now look, she'd been caught wearing his clothing again. She felt the heat of flush rise over her shoulders and up her neck.

Mack leaned a shoulder against the open jamb and smiled, looking more piratical than ever. Could be the night's events mixing with the scruff on his dark chin, lending to the general impression. Still, with his curls in disarray, dirt staining his trousers and long coat, and dark eyes that raked her with a knowing look, he looked every inch the captain of the ship, in charge of all and everyone on board.

Flora hadn't the coyness of her mother, but she understood the glint of lust all too well. What surprised her was her reaction. Suddenly, Flora became all too aware of his thin shirt and nothing else. Acting on impulse, she stretched languidly, enjoying the fluidity of her muscles. The soft cotton drifted off her shoulder.

Mack straightened and kicked the door closed with the heel of his boot. His fist anchored to his hip. "I wonder if you use your claws."

Flora felt her brows shoot into her hairline.

"Someone said you're like a cat with nine lives..." His deep voice lowered to a sultry purr of his own, the words coming slow. The very syllables washed over her like a velvet touch. "All your near misses. And now, seeing you here on my bunk, in my shirt, looking for all intents like a prize to be won, I have to wonder...do you scratch?"

Though never a participant, Flora knew this game. Understood the rules and, more importantly, the stakes. The question only remained of whether she wanted to play.

Her body answered for her. Nipples grazing the worn soft cotton craved a touch she'd never known.

As though reading her reaction, Mack's eyes drifted lower, to the open neckline, before returning to capture her gaze with his dark intent.

She blinked several times in an attempt to muster words. Flora swallowed. "I thought you said women curse ships."

He narrowed the distance and stepped closer. As he leaned in, a muscled arm bracketing either side of her body, fingers splayed across the mattress, she felt absorbed by the depth of his eyes. At this range she could identify the subtle shading between the black pupil and deep brown.

"And here's the proof that they do," he responded, his lips a breath away from her own. "While I should be concentrating on the next steps, how to get into the cave and retrieve what's mine, I have become distracted."

A warm glow suffused her body. "Is that all that's yours?"

"Everything on this ship is mine." His finger reached up to trace a line from her ear, over her neck, and along her collarbone. "This cabin...this bunk..." He tugged the shirt farther down her shoulder until her breast almost sprang free. "This shirt."

A shiver racked her, and she closed her eyes and tilted her head back to the cushion beneath. As she anticipated, his lips followed his touch. Delicious tendrils of pleasure coursed along her every nerve ending. The combined effect of soft lips and harsh stubble starting at her shoulder and slowly moving up her neck tightened her stomach, causing a throbbing deep within her being. Her breath hitched when his lips at last claimed hers.

Unsure of what to do next, Flora lay as still as her quivering body would allow. "Me?"

Mack's rough palm caressed her cheek. "Everything," he said against her ear. "On this ship." He nibbled the lobe and a great ball of fire gathered in her loins. "Is mine."

Unable to resist further, Flora reached to enmesh her fingers in the thick nest of his dark hair and pulled his lips back to her. "Yes," she breathed against his mouth.

Then, like the cold ocean waves which had tried to claim her only days before, Mack stood, his hands back on his hips. "Yes," he echoed. "But not now."

"Not now?" she asked stupidly, scrabbling back to sitting position.

"All in good time, my bounty," Mack said, pulling the shirt up over her shoulders. "But for now, I need your help, and we can not afford such languid distractions."

"My help?"

"Yes."

He stroked her hair back from her brow and smiled. Another light replaced the glint of lust. Amusement? Was he laughing at her?

"No," he said and kissed her forehead. "I'm not laughing at you, nor do I take what you offer lightly. But I need you in a different way just now."

Flora sprang away from his touch and up onto her knees. "How do you do that?" Her breath came in jagged little gasps. "Stop doing that."

Mack laughed, the sound joyous like she'd never heard before. "Your innocence is a refreshment."

Now Flora laughed. "Innocence is no' something I've been confused with."

"Perhaps not," he said and turned from her to his desk. "But that doesn't mean it's not true. As we both know, you're no doxy, and everything you think shows clearly on your face."

Flora cupped her cheeks and felt the heat sear her grip.

"You're certainly not what first impressions may have alluded."

"Am I not?"

He laughed again and took a seat at his desk. Pulling the leather scraps of the map from his pocket, he laid them flat, then picked up the paper Flora had illustrated for him that morning of the details of the treasure cave. "Well, perhaps I'd be more accurate to say you are more than what you first seemed to be."

Flora spread her fingers and gaped between, watching the broad expanse of his back as he leaned over the etching. She allowed the glow of his praise to wash away the feeling of rejection from moments ago.

"And you need me?"

He tossed her a meaningful look over his shoulder, and she felt the fiery quickening again. "In more ways than one."

Chapter Twenty-One

The girl's eyes consumed her face. Like those of an animal about to be slaughtered, the orbs rolled, taking in everything and nothing at the same time. Even as she set foot on the rough planks of the longboat, her face held a greenish hue beneath the pale skin. This added to the almost transparent impression of the skull beneath. He wondered how much, other than swimming into the cave entrance by way of the cliffs, she had taken in.

Purple lined her bloodless lips despite the sun now well up and warming their backs. The same lips that had aroused him almost beyond all sense but hours before.

If only there had been time.

It had hit Mack like a hammer of thunder coming out of a clear blue sky to enrage the sea to a deadly foam. Waiting for low tide was as much of a trap as all the other pitfalls they had overcome to find the treasure. The two distinct maps, one not working without the other. The beach. The rocks. The trench. The God-be-damned oak tree. That cunning Blackbeard knew his foe well—very well indeed.

"You can swim," he said above the creak of the longboat bumping against the *Navigator* as they gained purchase to heave to.

How he loved the sounds of the rhythmic dip and slap of the oars. It wouldn't take them long to move closer to where the cave entrance should be, though now submerged in the high tide. He glanced from the approaching rock face to Flora. Perhaps if she talked, she would lose the cast of the ghost. "Somewhat at least. I saw you."

If he followed his gut, the task at hand would require three to enter the cave from the sea, from the cliff face, and one left in the longboat. Blackbeard had counted on the general sailor's aversion to swimming. Mack knew this as sure as his own name. That he could swim and enjoyed the exercise was an anomaly his men generally regarded as supernatural. Burke, Mack realized during his scheming, could also swim, but, be damned, he needed the man's skills at the helm. The *Navigator* had to be close without succumbing to the rocks. The longboat would drop anchor, and Mack trusted Tiller to keep a careful watch.

And…if he were correct, he needed someone slight and agile like the girl for the netting. Someone who wouldn't disturb the fragile rigging of the planks.

Finally, her gaze focused on his, and he noted the firebrand girl returning, clear in the depths of her eyes. "Swim, yes," she said, her hands gripping the bench with such force her knuckles whitened. "But I'm no fish. I canna breath under the depths. Nor, do I think, can you."

He laughed, more relieved by the heat of her reply than what she said. He needed the tenacious girl who had challenged him on the beach and demanded to be brought along on this most current adventure. He needed the fighter from the docks who had noticed every detail and planned her survival accordingly. He needed the woman…

"Red here, though." Mack pointed a thumb over his shoulder at the lad with the other set of oars. "He all but has gills. Isn't that right, Red."

"As you say, Capt'in." The boy grinned, revealing a snaggle-toothed smile. "On the beaches of Cornwall, me ol' da threw us in the waves afore we could walk. Sink or swim, he'd say."

"Sink or swim, aye," Mack echoed.

Flora shrugged, looking less than convinced of his plan.

Mack lifted the rope. "We'll be tied together."

"If you wait for low tide…"

Her fear had clouded her previous perception. Anger and impatience flared. Sweat ran in rivulets down his back. They were nearing the halfway mark. He couldn't fight with her when they were at the face. Time was a commodity he couldn't afford to waste. He had no idea how long it would take, once inside, to secure the load, or even if he could secure it all at once. All crewmen were required to be on point to pull this off. This now included Flora.

"By the devil." He pounded a fist to the bench.

She straightened and focused on his face.

"What?"

She said this with her old insolence, and he grinned.

Seeming to forget her fear, still gripping the seat, she leaned forward. "Are ye gone suddenly daft?"

"I may be," he responded by leaning in so only she could hear. "'Tis because of you if I am."

Color flared like dewy petals on her cheeks. He had her attention now. "'Tis you who caught the trap," he began.

Her gaze refocused. "What trap?"

"If we wait 'til low tide, the loot will be lost to the depths of the ocean," he said, softening his tone and brushing his hair back under his hat. "'Tis you who said you didn't know how deep the water beneath. Said it looked like leviathan homeland, if I remember correctly."

She shrugged, but he noticed how her interest had diverted the fear and she had loosened her grip on the bench.

"You said as much yourself, and I hadn't caught it at first, being too consumed in the contents and the details of the cave itself—"

"All seemed too easy," she said, excitement pitching her tones. "Yes."

She had released her death grip on the seat and slapped her thigh. He glanced quickly at the shape and curve of the limb as good as revealed in the damp fabric. Not to be outdone by his growing longing, he returned his gaze to her face and tried to put their brief moment in his cabin from his mind. Time enough—

The cliff face seemed to be clawing toward them instead of the other way around.

"So we set the net," she continued. "Attach the rigging, and have the *Navigator* pull 'er free."

"There's my girl," he said and had to refrain from pulling her into his arms and kissing her blind. Had he ever imagined finding his match in a woman? "Easier planned than commenced."

Flora lowered her head. "I bob more than swim and...I be...be..."

Mack took her freezing hand in his. "These late summer currents are warmer than even the earlier part of the season," he said, trying to make his voice reassuring. "There'll be an air pocket. I am sure of it. Has to be, actually."

When her brow furrowed, he elaborated.

"The trench by which you found the opening." He released her hand and mimed. "That will suction off the water, leaving the ceiling free. A place for us to breathe, and I have a float buoy."

"But how long from when we go under until we reach the grotto? We've no light."

He glanced from their position to the *Navigator*, and then to the island. The entrance should be revealed more from feel than from sight. He could only estimate they were close. From this distance he could just see the top of the tall oak tree. Surely, the water undulating back and forth through the cave and into the trench should snag the small boat in the wake and current. Tiller's job would be to hold the longboat far enough away to keep it from wrecking against the craggy face and close enough for them to be able to get back to it quickly.

"Part of the trap, as I see it," Mack said, pointing below. "That rancid Teach would have had to work by the same conditions."

"But why?" Her question sounded more innocent than he would have expected from someone who had been so exposed to the underbelly of society as she had as a street rat.

"You must have heard of ol' Blackbeard?"

At this, both Tiller and Red also leaned in to hear the telling. Their oars continued their fluidity of motion, yet they had adjusted their seats to be closer. Mack shook his head and chuckled. "Well, if we must away with the man's treasure, a moment more to understand our foe will be worth the effort, I suppose."

Like all men of the sea, they appreciated a good story, whether they had heard it all before or not. "Edward Teach's history with the sea sometimes seems to date back to when Noah first learned to sail."

Mack waited for their chuckling to subside. "The paper you found..." He pointed at Flora. "Only confirmed what we all suspected. He'd once been, as I am sure we've all been at one time, under his majesty's flag. Though an English commander, a more vile creature never roamed the ocean since the dreaded kraken.

"Teach earned his name when he refused to be wigged and shaved. Grew his beard as thick and black as the devil himself—"

"Much like our good capt'in," Red quipped, caught himself, and sputtered, "Beg pardon, sir. A goodlier commander there's never-a been."

Mack laughed and slapped the boy on the back. "No offense, lad. 'Tis too true my beard be just as thick and black, and we be after his treasure, but unlike that black heart, I'll not be a-killing my crew for a few bob."

"No, sir," Tiller said. "What we take, we share."

They were almost to the edge of the cliff face. "Anything would set that treacherous bastard off. He would provoke a fight and then get them with a blade he carried up his sleeve. A quick jab through the abdomen, slicing upward through the body cavity, he would ensure that his opponent would surely die. He had no honor. He'd weave trophies into his beard."

Here Mack tickled the ends of his own stubbled

chin and was rewarded with the rounded O of her soft mouth. Such a distraction.

"Someone that disreputable could rely on no one, and so he'd have to be able to get to the grotto by himself. Certainly, he wouldn't be worming his way in each and every time he needed to fill his purse or to add to the treasure. And for that reason, I am counting on our ability to gain access."

"You're thinking there'll be some sort of light source?" she asked. "That daylight will be reflected inside?"

"Precisely."

Flora nodded. "Yes."

"Yes?"

"The one thing I have learned these last weeks is to trust in our good captain," she said, her eyes sincere.

Each of the oarsmen nodded vigorously and said, "Aye, that he is."

"I've been in there with but a lantern," she said as they bumped up against the cliff face. "Yet the place glowed as though waiting for me. What you say could work."

Chapter Twenty-Two

The small anchor clattered overboard, and despite the heat, Flora had to clamp her teeth to keep them from chattering. Her experience with the ocean featured very little swimming and more frolicking in the waves as they bumped up against the shoreline. She knew enough to keep her head above water and get back to the beach, yet she never had waded out farther than necessary to test her endurance.

"Tiller." The captain addressed the gangly youth Flora had come to view as a friend. "You're all eyes."

"Aye," he said. "As directed."

The dory bumped up against the cliff face, and Flora struggled with the urge not to make a leap to cling to the rocks and try to scramble to the top and what promised safety from the hungry ocean. Entering the maw underwater seemed only like an invitation to an early demise. Visions of the storm and being sucked under, having no breath, threatened to consume her.

Mack handed a faded green buoy to her and one to Red. "Here." His eyes burrowed into hers, and his hand skimmed the tops of hers and stilled. His thumb stroked the tender skin between wrist and palm. His normally dark gaze softened, and Flora felt caressed.

She tried to smile, and his lip hooked up slightly at the edge. "Good enough," he said and bent to the netting at his feet.

The crusted slime on the edge of the buoy turned her stomach. She swallowed back the phlegm. Certainly, she'd seen worse. This was no time to be squeamish.

She opened her mouth to speak, closed it, swallowed hard, and tried again. "How will we be able to get under the rim with the floaters?"

Mack tilted his head to the side, glancing from her to where they hoped was the cave entrance. Then he lifted the bulk of netting. "You see, they're not that heavy. They'll float enough to hold up the net, but will easily submerge and offer little resistance," he said, illustrating with his hands. "Cord ends will be tied to the boat. We'll drop the net to the bottom and take the other two ends with us into the grotto."

The captain scanned the area from the rock face back to the ship. "Based on your illustrations, we should be able to wrap the net around the treasure and haul the buoyed ends back out with us."

Flora and Red nodded. She could picture the plan, but not her part in it.

"Then we'll haul the buoys back to the ship, and the *Navigator* will pull the treasure free of the fittings. With any luck, we'll lose little in the process, so long as we can try to keep the chests closed."

Mack removed his shirt, revealing a long, lean torso much lighter than the tanned neck and forearms she was used to seeing. Lifting a length of rope, he draped it cross-body from his neck to under his arm. He pointed at Flora. "And that's where you come in. Someone small enough to not disturb the pilings but strong enough to fasten the rope in place until we're ready."

Flora felt her brow pucker.

Mack nodded and bent to remove his boots. "Then we'll wrap the whole with the net."

"Just like that?" Red asked.

Mack smiled a youthful grin she'd never seen before. "Just like that." And he snapped his fingers. With another length of cord, retrieved from the bow of the boat, he wrapped his arms around her middle and threaded the length around her and tied it in the front. Taking the long end with plenty of slack in between, he looped the other end around his own waist.

Terror tightened her windpipe, and Flora struggled to draw breath. She blinked several times. "That'll take some time. I told ye, I'm no fish."

He patted her leg, and her body trembled. "And I told you, there'll be air pockets."

Without further chatter, Mack jumped overboard and the rope around her middle tightened but didn't pull her over.

On cue, Red stood, removed his shirt, tightened the rags of his breeches, and with a grin bespoke of adventure to come, dove into the depths. In a moment, his face bobbed to the surface and he launched up to the side of the dory, elbows butterflied to hold his position. "Toss me the buoy ends," he commanded of Tiller.

Red turned his face to her. "'Tis great and refreshing on such a warm day," he said. "Come on, now. Faster in, faster done, and richer we all are."

"Here, here," Tiller said. "Go on now, girlie. You'll be just fine. Capt'in says you'll be fine, you'll be fine."

"And I say what I mean and mean what I say," Mackenzie said, surfacing on the other side of the boat.

"This side, now, so you don't crack your head on the rocks. There're some jagged ends under the surface."

Flora tied the hem of her shirt firmly under her breasts and ensured her pants would hold. She hadn't worn shoes, and nothing else needed doing to prolong her delay. She knew if she dallied longer, he'd surely lose patience. She dipped her hand in the water and shivered. Not as cold as she recalled, but certainly not warm.

"Best to just jump in all at once and get the shock of it over with," he said.

She'd stared down the barrel of a gun before, so this should not be causing her such tension. Grinding her teeth, Flora jumped. Colors danced behind closed lids, and the taste of salt filled her mouth. She broke the surface, spluttering and cursing.

"There you are," Mack said with a grin. "I was worried there for a moment."

Flora tried not to smile as she blinked the seawater from her vision. "All right, let's get on with it then."

"Tiller," Mack said, "hold the net until I locate the entrance."

He pivoted in the water like some dolphin and addressed Flora. "Hold to the side of the boat and move to the bow. You'll feel the line pull a bit, but hold tight until I surface. We may need to position the boat better to be closer to the entrance. I'll see what I find."

Flora followed his instructions while he dove beneath the small crests of waves. The slack of rope tickled down her legs, then pulled away from her body. She watched a shadow move beneath the surface to the face of the cliff.

Red splashed alongside. "Best to conserve our

energy, me thinks."

Flora nodded, taking great gulps of air for all that Mack wasn't breathing while she waited for him to come up.

Then he burst onto the surface. "It's right there." He tossed his head and water flew in all directions from the mass of dark curls. "Ease out the netting as we move off, Tiller. Slow and steady. We don't need to be weighted down unnecessarily."

"Aye."

Tiller handed Flora the buoy while Mack adjusted the length of spare rope from his neck. "No need for this to choke me, either."

Red snickered. "That'd be the sure thing to deprive ye of the pleasure of the treasure."

Mack barked a laugh. "'Twould indeed." One heavily muscled forearm hanging to the edge of the boat, he turned to Flora. "One step at a time, now. Take our time and trust me to lead. All right?"

Flora bobbed a nod, her mouth too dry, her tongue suddenly too thick to form words.

"We'll float to the rocks, and then we'll go together," he said and yelled across to Red, who smiled as bright as the sun overhead, eager for the coming adventure. "Keep close, ye hear me, lad?"

Flora tried to be as optimistic, imagining the stories they would tell the others, and failed.

Mack's dripping fingers gripped her chin, and he looked directly into her eyes. "Big breaths now. In and out. Fill yer lungs as much as possible. In and out...that's right."

In a moment, they were touching the slate face of the wall. "Big gulps now. All right. Ready. Here we go." Then he was gone, and Flora felt the rope start to wind away from her body. She had no choice but to follow. He'd pull her with him either via the tug on the line or voluntarily.

She looked to the sky and squinted into the brightness. Taking one last breath, she allowed herself to sink and drew the buoy with her, hugging it tight to her body with one arm, while using her other as a paddle. She kicked her feet fiercely to move forward in the direction she imagined the captain had disappeared. Succumbing to the instant quiet, she forced her eyes open, pleased it wasn't as dark as she had fancied it would be. Quite the opposite. The sun's rays seeped into the depths in radiant angles beaming into the depths. Following the lead of the line, she saw the swift figure of Mack ahead. He stopped and looked back at her, waving his hand to direct her to him.

In seconds, she and Red hovered just in front of the captain, feet below the surface, with the cave entrance now visible. He pointed and then moved off, his muscled arms carrying him forward with swift motion, the netting spinning like a spider web behind them.

Instead of gloom and an inability to navigate, the grotto seemed to have captured the sun's filtered rays. Scanning the inside, Flora spotted flat mirrored panels anchored in the depths. These reflective circles bounced the light up from the entrance and directed the light into the cave.

Her lungs ached, and she started to panic, unable to focus or care what she was supposed to do. She needed to return to the boat. She needed the real light of day—land—air. She turned blindly, moving back from the direction they had just traversed. She'd return or not, nothing was worth drowning. She'd escaped once and wouldn't give the ocean a second chance.

The link between her and Mack tightened and pulled her forward. She fought against the tug, but like an anchor, the rope hauled her down. Flora opened her mouth to scream and tasted the sea water. She shook her head and wrapped both arms around the buoy.

"No," bubbled out of her lips never to be heard, yet the word screamed in her mind.

Suddenly arms wrapped around her, and her head broke free of the sea's watery grip.

Flora gagged and coughed, shaking with a lethal mixture of fear, relief, and dread.

"Shush," a strong voice said in her ear. "You're all right."

One strong muscled arm held her to him while the other weaved with the water holding them up. "We're almost there."

"I can see it, Capt'in," Red said, excitement raising the octave of his youthful voice. "'Tis right below. I sees it."

"Aye, lad," Mack said. "It is, indeed."

His warmth and confidence traveled through Flora, and she looked at him and nodded.

"There, lass, we're almost there," he said, squeezing her to him. "You're our lucky charm, and nothing ever happens to the lucky charm. Isn't that right, Red."

"'Tis too true," he said, bobbing close.

"Now we need a light and agile touch to secure the caskets and then wrap the netting," he said, pointing below. "When you need air, just swim up. But remember, the faster we're done, the sooner we're out of here and rich men, all—and you too, lass."

"Yes," she croaked, then nodded. The depth wasn't far, and the ability to gain access to air gave her courage. He was right. This could be done. Flora imagined what ol' Maggs would say. This was their chance—her chance to achieve what her mother had never been able to give her. She felt the strength return to her limbs. "Yes. I can do this."

"Good lass."

Chapter Twenty-Three

The trio bobbed and weaved, up and down, from the air pocket to the treasure chests directly below, like dolphins playing in their pods. In the murky depths Mack noticed what made him cringe. In fact, he had hoped his plan would prove to be an easy procedure. He could see this was not to be.

Damn his crew to their eyeballs for their general aversion to swimming. That they could believe such an old wives' tale, that not knowing how to swim didn't challenge the sea gods and they would spare you a watery death, or if they must take you, it would somehow be quicker. Filling his aching lungs, now he had to wonder if the three of them could possibly bring the plan to fruition.

From what Flora had described and her incredibly accurate sketches, he knew only within the weightlessness of the ocean would they be able to secure the chests without the whole ancient apparatus dissolving under their ministrations. Mack could easily see how when Flora had stepped from the trench, it barely held her additional burden. No wonder she had been so shaken. He really couldn't fathom the depth of the water below, so black were the depths beneath the mirrored plates. Now he wished he'd brought the lead line measure.

On hindsight, he could have snatched at least one

of the chests before the antique underpinnings gave way, but then he'd have walked away from enough wealth to set him and the crew up for life. Born with the gambler's mindset of all merchant sailors, he couldn't walk away from all that was now within his grasp—a lifetime of security. He could sail for pleasure, set up his own merchant line, build a legacy for generations to come.

Finalizing the last loop around the chest, Mack swam under Flora's feet to emerge next to her. He clutched a soggy tree root above his head to rest from the constant exertion and hold him afloat. He scanned her face. Despite the circumstance of how they had met, despite their age difference, there was no question of his attraction. Never one to lie to himself, he saw she was his match in every way he could have imagined for a wife. She'd never hold him back, yet she'd challenge both his wit and intellect. He found he respected her. He shook his head at the notion. Still, what she lacked, in breeding and connections for the society he sought, they could surely purchase with Black's gold.

Catching his breath in the heavy air thick with pungent scents of the soil and roots prevalent in this part of the grotto's wall, he gazed up at the unseamed rock ceiling. Stalactites gnashed like bared teeth back at him. Some of the more superstitious of his crew would never have made it a moment in the grotto even if they could swim.

And like sand in the hourglass, through the tide, the sea sucked back the depths. Time was slipping away from them quickly. Mack saw the shadow of the trench entrance from the land side of the cave completely submerged and marveled at the mind which had created such an enclosure to protect his treasure. Still, he didn't know what to do about the under pilings. He had hoped after securing the chests to simply wrap the netting around the ledge and have the *Navigator* pull the bulk free. But the additional weight and posts might prevent even the ship from being able to pull it free without causing the cave-in of the entire grotto, burying the treasure forever out of everyone's reach.

"Damn." He slapped a palm against the water.

"What?" Flora and Red both turned, each holding a buoy and panting. Even in the dimness, he could see their lips were blue-rimmed, their eyes bloodshot. They were running out of time in more ways than one.

He pointed to the shelf. "Any thoughts?"

Flora bit her lip, jaw muscles tight as she tried to control the chatter. "You wanted to take the net from below and loop it over so we could swim the buoys out without being caught in the netting?"

Mack um-hummed. "Aye."

"So now we do the opposite...loop from top to underneath."

"Bloody dangerous, that," Red said, his freckles more pronounced in his blue-cast, pale face. "Lost my dad to a tangle in a fishing net."

Mack nodded. "Red's right," he said. "'Tis one thing to swim above the weight and take it out. Quite another to go under... Damnation, it'd be like trying to avoid octopus tentacles."

"So we just leave it?" She splayed her fingers and fanned out her arm. "All this work, all this effort for naught? Do you really think Tommy Two-Guns will give up so easily?"

Mack's blood ran hot at the suggestion of failure

compared to such a lowlife. In anger he reefed on the weight of the netting attached to the buoy. He'd hardly any strength to lift it free of the surface. "If we do this, once we go under, each swim to the wall and break the surface. I'll feed the bulk over until it is surrounded."

Her teeth continued to chatter and her eyes looked frightened, yet he watched her shoulders set. She nodded and reached out a hand to Red. "We c-can d-d-do th-h-is," she said. "You s-said y-you were born to s-swim, R-red."

The boy's thin mouth lifted marginally at one end. "If you're in, I'm there too."

Then he turned to Mack. "Lucky charm, right, Capt'in?"

"That's right, lad." He motioned below them. "You need to go under the ledge and between the foundations, being sure not to disrupt the chests. We can't take the chance of them falling free before they're secured by the netting. There's no way for any of us to dive down and retrieve them in this murk."

"Aye," Red said.

"We must move swiftly now." Mack referenced with a head nod toward the waterline and the top of the trench entrance becoming visible. "We're out with the tide."

Red swam to the other side, buoy pushed ahead of him. Mack turned to Flora. "Take no chances." He cupped her trembling chin. "Keep to the plan...you hear?"

She nodded.

Mack swam to the middle of the grotto, feeling the pull of the current toward the cave entrance. Stronger and stronger was the tide. He had to push ever harder, his leg muscles burning, to stay afloat. A chill had set in and tingled at his spine, sapping his energy. But it wouldn't be long now. Still, he glanced to either side, where both Flora and Red waited for his signal, and wondered how they were holding up, each so much smaller than he.

He tugged the netting from both sides until the cone end was bunched and the headline buoys floated in from the cave entrance, where their rope leads were tied to the dory. He caught his foot in one of the square, knitted openings and floundered, taking in a mouthful of seawater. He sputtered and spat, cursing himself.

"You all right, Capt'in?"

"Aye, lad," he said, swimming so he hovered over the ledge, careful now not to disrupt the contents with his long legs. The water had descended so fast that, if he wanted, he could easily stand on the tops of the chests. But he dared not and pushed the weight of the cone end over the desired spot.

"Yes," he called, and his voice echoed throughout the chamber. "Now."

As he watched them each take their end of the headline under and between, he let the burden of the cone end drop, only noticing as it fell that Flora's buoy had gotten tangled in one of the underpilings which stuck down from the ledge and between the rickety beams. Horrorstruck, he watched the net descend and take her down with it.

"No!" he yelled as air bubbles danced to the surface.

Chapter Twenty-Four

Had Flora not looked up just as the net was falling through the water, the weight of the impact would have knocked out of her what little air she had in reserve. Instead, she wrapped her arms tight around the buoy, rounded her shoulders, tucked her head, and took the impact on the curve of her back. With a clarity she didn't know she possessed, in the flash of seconds, she knew not to fight against the net, it only had so much line. She'd fall with it and with any luck be able to untangle and reach the surface.

Her lungs burned, and she fought the instinct to breath in. She looked up, wondering how she'd make it back to the surface. Then her feet hit the bottom. Unlike their original estimates, the water proved shallow. A fathom, maybe two, below the pilings. The captain would like that. If they lost any of the chests, they could be retrieved, especially at low tide.

She reached above and tried to move the bulk of the net, but it was so heavy, and the more she moved the more tangled she became. Her body convulsed. She clamped a hand over her nose and mouth to prevent the natural instinct to suck for air which no longer existed. Fear gripped her. Only survival mattered.

Flora clenched her fists, fighting the numbness and blurred vision. White spots danced before her eyes. She had been saved once from this watery grave. How could she ever hope to survive a second time?

Again she bent her knees and struggled to break free of the bonds by springing upright. She had no energy. She was so cold and tired. Already she could imagine barnacles forming on her skeleton as she slept forever beneath Black's gold.

"Help me!" she cried out and felt the first rush of water hit her neglected lungs. So empty of air, they accepted the foreign substance as though it belonged there. Her hands drifted to the sides and she felt as light as an air bubble. Surely her mother and father were waiting for her. She'd see her brother again. It had been so long.

Then she thought of the captain. He'd been a good man. Kinder than she could have imagined. He'd had no reason to take her on board she knew now. He could have stolen the map from her and been on his way. Yet he seemed to have humored her. Then he had saved her when everyone else would have let her go, a casualty of an ocean storm. The same fate met by so many of the sea. Then he talked to her and seemed to respect her opinion.

Perhaps, had time been on their side, he would have come to see her as a woman. Perhaps...

She closed her eyes, accepting her fate. Leaning into the surrounding netting, she allowed it to wrap around her like a blanket and take her to the sea bottom. As she began to settle, she felt the impact of another object on top of her. Had one of the chests fallen? The captain wouldn't be pleased.

As the last of her resources abandoned her to her grave, she was jostled from her nest. Arms gripped her and tugged around both her waist and her legs. Then her head slammed against rock while a fist smashed against her back. Soon she would be free from this pain. Soon she would be with her family again and forget the heartache of leaving a man she knew she could have loved.

Voices called through the fog, and she strained to hear. She wanted to call out that she was coming. She'd be with Maggs soon, and they'd laugh as they had when she was a child and free of the burden of the streets and having to thieve and watch her mother's beauty fade in the hostility of the lust of men incapable of real affection.

Her body convulsed, and she registered this with more awareness than she had expected while dying. The voices grew louder and more aggressive, echoing around her, while she struggled to return to the oblivion calling to her.

"Breathe, God damn it."

The voice was harsh, angry, and familiar. Mack.

"Does she breathe, lad?"

Flora felt the tickle of an ear next to her lips. They had gotten her free. They had pulled her from the depths. She struggled to open heavy eyelids. Her body refused to listen, and she felt powerless to assist the fight to save her own life. How easy to just slip away.

"I think—"

"You think," Mack yelled. His voice came back to her, worried, edging on panic. "What?"

"There's life, Capt'in." Red's voice invaded her consciousness. "A faint wheeze—yes—yes. There's breath."

Strong arms wrapped around her tightly, squeezing, and she felt the beat of his heart against her chest. "Come now, lass," he said close to her ear in a voice she had never heard him use before. Was that a slight shakiness? "Don't go on and give that ol' Davey Jones all your sass. We've plenty of sparring here to keep you right prickly."

"Her eyes, Capt'in," Red said, an anxious note to his tone. "You see there…a flutter."

"You're right, lad. I see it too."

Flora felt a gentle touch on her cheeks. Her skin responded, and a flutter filled her belly, heating her from the depths of her being.

"Come now, lass, no amount of gold can replace you. Don't go on. Stay a while."

Other than to her mother, Flora had been a burden for so much of her life. His need of her, the obvious longing in his words, tone, and touch would have choked her further if she'd been capable. She'd never viewed men in this light before. Having next to no memory of her father or brother other than the stories told by Maggs, the species offered no mystery, only a means to an end. A way to generate income through subterfuge, then theft.

She had to see this for herself to confirm she'd not died and was somehow imagining the man she longed for also wanted her. She struggled to open her lids, the effort rendering her limp with spent energy. Her teeth began to chatter again. Then all sentimental imaginings were stalled as Flora was wracked with waves of coughing. She felt as though her body were splintering away, yet muscled arms held her close.

"That's right, Flora," he said softly into her ear, patting her back. "Get it all out."

"She's doin' it, Capt'in," Red said excitedly.

"She's come back from the deep."

"Twice."

Within moments, bright light filtered through her vision, and she was hoisted over the side of the dory. From one set of arms to another, rough hands settled her in the bottom and wrapped a blanket over her shivering form. Then Tiller's wide mouth smiled down at her.

"There now, lass, lie still," he said. The dory rocked and bumped against the cliff face. "We'll be back on board in no time now."

She opened her mouth to ask about the chests, but nothing came out but a lungful of sea water, which dribbled down her chest as another wave of coughing overtook her.

"Easy, lass," Tiller said. "They'll be back."

With all her remaining strength, she reached for the side of the boat and hauled herself up to peer over the edge, catching sight of two bobbing heads as they swam beneath the overhang of the now-visible cave entrance.

"Too dangerous," she croaked.

"Nonsense," Tiller said, tutting against his teeth. The sound reminded her of an old woman, and he furthered this notion when he eased her, with applied pressure on her shoulders, back into the bottom of the boat. The gentle motion lulled her exhausted body toward a slumber she fought. "Capt'in said you did all the hard work. They're just off to retrieve the buoys, and we'll take 'em back to the ship. By the turn of the tide, we're all as rich as Poseidon hisself."

Flora slumped back. Could it be true? Had they succeeded? Would they be as rich as the king himself?

She must have dozed, as it seemed only a heartbeat

had passed when the boat startled her awake, rocking perilously, waves sloshing over the sides. Two buoys bounced over the side, landing at her feet as she struggled up from her nest. The sun beat down, and she woke eager and excited, warmed through with the thought of her survival and the revelation of the captain's attention.

Mack's strong, muscled arm wrapped around the wooden edge of the boat, and then his broad grin outshone the impact of the sun. The boat dipped and heaved with the added weight. "There you are, lass."

Like a landed fish, Red splashed over the side and came to sit opposite. "I've never heard the likes of someone like you," he said with a shake of his head. Taking the buoys, he added the other two floats and tied them off, weighting the stern close to the watermark. "To fall to the hands of the drink twice and come out alive and well." He shrugged and shook his head again.

"'Tis the lucky charm," Tiller supplied, standing to assist the captain into the dory.

"And our Midas touch," Mack said, shaking his head like a shaggy dog, droplets flying from his heavy curls. "Thanks to you, lass, we did it."

Just then Tiller stood tall and pointed. "Not yet, we haven't," he said, his face losing the rosy tint it normally carried. "Sails rounding the island."

Chapter Twenty-Five

"By the blood," Mack shouted. "Blow the whistle. Alert the crew. To the guns. Unfurl the sails!"

All three men took up the oars and struggled with the additional weight, fighting the tide. "Tiller. Give the lead line. We'll have the ship assume the weight."

They must have spotted the ship prior to the piercing whistle blasts Tiller loosed. Mack watched his crew with pride as they assumed their positions and the anchor lifted from its mooring. In moments, the gun doors opened and the ship began closing the distance separating them. His heart pounded and sweat poured from his brow and stung his vision more than the saltwater quickly evaporating off his skin and clothes in the exertions, replaced by a solid sheen of perspiration.

His arms burned, but the previous exhaustion from swimming and diving was forgotten. He needed to protect more than the treasure now dragging on the bottom behind them. Mack knew only too well what would happen to Flora should they be boarded. Worse still, if this were the banker Tommy Two-Guns and his devious crew of misfits, they'd have little compunction over their actions when it came to her and how she'd obtained the map in the first place.

He looked over his shoulder and spared a glance for Flora, who at the moment returned his gaze, eyes bright and eager. She'd taken up an oar and pulled harshly through the current, her face flushed and her mouth set. She smiled a feral snarl and almost growled at him. "They'll not take us so long as I draw breath."

Mack felt his eyes widen and had to look away to hide his answering grin. Wasn't that his line? He whooped as they bumped against the *Navigator* and he bounded up the rope ladder. The crew heaved the dory up, and all were quickly hauled aboard, the buoy lines wrapped securely around the fittings.

"Lower the canvas. Secure the net," he shouted to Hemsley and whistled for Duke, who came bounding. "Get the chests on board."

He spared but a moment to scratch the dog's head before running to the foredeck, where he climbed the mast. Burke held the helm and sent him a salute. Mack nodded and continued to monkey climb to the crow's nest. The wavery line on the horizon came into view. Approaching fast, the three-master had all sheets crisp in the wind. Six of his crew, including Red and Tiller, struggled with the weight of the chests.

He scuttled down the mast and ran back to the gunners. "We'll get 'em on the broadside when they open their ports to fire on us," he shouted to the gunners. "Wait for my signal."

Then he returned to the net. "Into the water, Tiller. Fish them up one at a time."

"What if we lose one?" Red asked, preparing to jump overboard.

Mack looked over the edge to where the net's contents hovered just below the surface. He turned to the assembly of youths. "Don't."

"Aye," they chorused.

Striding to the main deck, he stood next to Burke,

who watched the progress of the loading of the chest. "What do you make of 'er?"

"She's no man-o-war ship, and she flies no flags," Burke responded. "Still, I no' like to be a sitting duck. I want the sheets up and to be away from here. Too easy to pin us in."

"Agreed," Mack answered, taking in all exits. "If we have to fight it out?"

"We outgun her, but that only counts if we can out-maneuver and be off," Burke said, pointing to the open gunnels on the approaching vessel. "She's on the move, and we're not. Added, she's the advantage of the wind."

"For now," Mack agreed and left the deck, his dog keeping stride as he bounded down the stairs to help the progress of the chests. "Keep the nose face-on. Give 'er nothing to fire upon."

"Aye," he said. "We're out of range, but they're closing fast. Though they'll have to slow in order to turn to fire."

"Then that's our signal. We'll fly canvas, turn, and fire. She'd be a fine prize, but we'll take the bounty we have and be away."

"Aye, Capt'in."

Back to the gunners, Mack gathered them to the rail. "Hoist and cant the guns on the forecastle, forward at the bow. You see there?" He pointed to the approaching vessel. "We'll splinter the masts."

Even from this distance, Mack saw his men outnumbered the crew of the attacker. Chances were, his were better trained, having spent all their time at sea in one skirmish after another, while this enemy ship was only deployed at the owner's discretion on a needs-only basis. Likely more imposing visually than practically.

"You're thinking they've not been tested," Hemsley said, striding up alongside Mack.

"Counting on it." He turned to the quartermaster. "All on board?"

A wide grin split the older man's weathered features. "Stowed below," he said. "Our girl saw to the full of it."

"Our girl?"

"The lass's as good a crew man as any sailor we've on board."

"By Christ, she is that," he agreed and slapped Hemsley on the back. "And we'll profit from it, too, once we're out of this fix."

"Aye, indeed."

"Hoist sails," Mack cried, turning to face the main deck. "To the wind. Narrow the field, ready the cannon."

The sheets caught with the sound of gunfire, and he bounded up the stairs as the ship gave a lurch forward. "Take us through the narrows," he commanded Burke. "We'll either lose them in the straights or crimple them in the process."

"Better to do both, eh, Capt'in," Burke shouted back, cramming his hat farther over his brow, shadowing the bulbous nose. What could be viewed of his manic expression looked more piratical than ever.

Just then an enemy cannonball struck the water dead ahead. Mack gripped the rail and swung out his spy glass. "Tiller to the crow's nest," he commanded. "Burke, keep in the wind, give 'er no target."

"Aye."

Raising his arm, he caught the eye of the master

gunner, then peered through his glass. The ship across the way offered its broadside as it went for the easy line of fire. Now was the time he'd waited for. "Light the fuse." Then he lowered his arm and slammed his fist into the wood. "Fire!"

The first ball took the pursuer's stern, blowing apart the large windows of the captain's quarters. The second volley crippled the foremast. A loud cheer erupted from the crew.

"No letting up, men," Mack shouted above the fray. "Adjust the angle. Bring 'er in tight. I want the next to the bow."

The enemy had twisted with the impact, only to their peril. The next volley struck the side and raked the length, setting off fires in its wake. The sails floundered with the combined impact of losing the wind and the crumbling of the foremast. This turned the ship farther, revealing the externally mounted rudder.

"Careful aim now, boys," he called. "You're to take the rudder. We want no pursuit."

"She'll be unsteerable," Flora said coming to stand beside him her face awash in excitement.

"That she will, lass."

"You'll not take her as a prize, then?"

Caught in the moment and uncaring of what his crew might think, he wrapped an arm about her shoulders and drew her to his side. "I've all the treasure a man could ever want." And he kissed her firmly on her lips.

She yielded to his touch, her lips giving and receiving. He felt the pull of her as true as the lure of the fight beckoned, both equally arousing.

Hand tangled in his hair, she broke the kiss, her

breath heaving. She pointed. "You crippled her."

A bellowing shout erupted.

"We're windward now. They'll never catch us. Take her through the narrows," Mack hollered.

"Aye. Through the narrows," Burke returned. "Then on to the straights."

"And then home," Mack said more quietly to Flora.

"Home?"

"Our home, if you'll have me."

"I've been yours from the moment we met."

"Aye, ye have," he said as they cleared their opponent's line of sight and left the view of fire and smoke behind. Then he swept her into his arms and, amongst the cheers of his crew, repeated, "Aye, ye have."

Here's a sneak peek into Book Two of the McGuire Series:

Bride by Proxy

by

Lori Power

Lori Power

Chapter One

1798

Garrett McGuire snapped the telescope closed, yet continued to peer into the clear night sky. The wind freshened off the inlet while he searched the stars. If asked, he couldn't say what he sought.

Answers?

Maybe.

To what questions?

What lay beyond what he couldn't see?

He drew a deep breath, and his heart mounted a bracing staccato. *Her.*

"The tide's right, Capt'in. Shall I light the signal?" Quartermaster Leonard Tippen asked as he climbed the steep stairs to the main deck. "All's quiet and no sign of patrols."

Reverie broken, Garrett's stare met Tippen's eyes in acknowledgment. He followed this with a nod and gave the heavens one last sweeping glance. The stars were so bright they smiled down, unperturbed in their eternity, like mini bonfires. Where were those celestial orbs when the *Isle Sky* had been fighting the spring storms crossing the Atlantic these last three weeks, he wondered. Fortunately, a new moon provided some cover tonight, and though the calm seas offered a welcome reprieve and a near tropical breeze, he would have preferred a slight fog this night to camouflage their presence in the open sea as they made their way into the secluded cove.

"One lantern, stern, three lifts," he ordered, turning his gaze toward the purple-shadowed land off the starboard bow. "Have the bosun's lad climb the mast to keep watch."

Though his father owned the fleet of merchant vessels and his family continued their fortune through shipbuilding, like his father before him, Garrett had chosen the sea over a life of business despite his father's best efforts. The unsettled whims of his mistress—the ocean—suited him fine. To appease her, ride her, live through her tantrums, and gratify her calm gave him purpose he could hardly articulate to anyone who did not share his affliction.

This choice did little to align him with his father's wishes even though Garrett could see his father yearned for the comforts at sea despite remaining in England these last years since his mother's death.

But Garrett differed. If he couldn't have the one "her" he desired, then he would stay in the bosom of this mistress who always welcomed him back.

His night-trained sight scanned the horizon, seeking the response. The sky was so clear that, within minutes of the signal being relayed, the return beacon blossomed visible for all to see.

Hands loose behind his back, Garrett strode to the railing. "We move with the tide. No need to fight what she freely gives." He turned to address the quartermaster, who then relayed the message through the chain of command. "We'll anchor in the usual position. Have the rowboats prepared to disembark. I'll go ashore with the first load."

"Aye, Capt'in."

With a practiced bound, Garrett leapt into the boat and assumed his position. A few strokes brought them to the shore. Knees bent, feet braced against the sides, ahead of the rowers, he stood as the skiff came aground on the pebbled sand. The beach had come alive, with lamps flickering like fireflies, marking a path for the sailors coming ashore. Stepping lightly, he jumped cleanly over the wooden side of the small boat used for such purposes of coming to land, leaving the vessel at anchor, and strode through the lapping waves, taking little heed of the water reaching to the cuff of his leather boots.

A portly man, flanked by two tired-looking fellows, stood just to the side, lamps raised to his approach. "In these most dangerous times, it's only a matter of time, my lad," Sir Francis Wiebe, merchant banker from Halifax-town said, shaking his head and smiling in greeting. "Even cats have only nine lives."

Garrett accepted the outstretched hand and shook it familiarly, a broad smile creasing his salt-licked features. "Ah, but it's to live those lives, and what a better way to live, eh, kind sir."

"Go on with your cheek." Sir Francis encased their clasped hands with his other, his natural affection overcoming the fear of the moment now that they were all ashore.

"'Tis providence, then, that I made it through yet again." Garrett dropped the gripped hands. "Yet your being here fools no one, Wiebe. 'Tis not concern for my well-being that pulls you from the comfort of bed and a well-rounded arse to warm it. Old miser that you are, you want to make good on your investment."

The older man laughed quietly, his palms covering the quaver of his ample stomach. Together, he and Garrett moved out of earshot of the other sailors and walked up the rocky bank, allowing the seamen to start unloading the cargo to the waiting wagons.

"You're too much like your father, you young rogue. And besides, who could blame me, my fine fellow?" Wiebe pulled at the lapels of his expensive fur-lined coat. "'Twas relief, true enough, when the messenger arrived to notify me of the signal. You were expected a fortnight ago. I have made one excuse after another for my being in this dreary part of the countryside and not back in my fine house in Halifax."

"An excuse to service your mistress well, you ol' scoundrel, nothing more," Garrett returned, sweeping up a handful of pebbles into his palm and tossing them one by one as he meandered up the hill. "Do not blame me for your extended pleasures."

Wiebe's face puckered, then split in a smile. The button-like eyes crinkled with mirth, and the light of mischief twinkled in their depths. "Do not distract me, now. We are on borrowed time, as you well know."

"Ah, but the cargo be worth your wait." Garrett patted the banker on the back. "Better delayed than not at all, when there is so much profit to be had, eh, old friend?"

"How you manage it…" Wiebe paused, then turned to watch the progress of the men on the beach.

Like many cogs in a precision clock, the seamen and laborers worked as an efficient unit. They progressed swiftly, moving the loaded longboats back and forth from ship to shore. "'Tis our good fortune the

British are, as has become custom for generations, so distracted by Napoleon's goings-on that a simple merchant like myself can smuggle a few barrels of our smoothest Scottish whisky and fine French brandy."

"Oh, har." Wiebe snagged his thumbs into the loops of his belt. "What about the Americans?"

"Weather, my old friend. Both friend and foe. The ol' bitch tossed us hither and to, promising we'd join the ghost ships of Sable Island this go round." Garrett gripped Wiebe's shoulder in a quick squeeze. "'Twas only a sound soothing. She relented to allow us passage."

"My word, you speak of the sea as though a living being."

Garrett turned to the sound of the waves lapping innocently at the beach as though never to bring any harm. He'd grown up with the stories of his parents' adventures at sea and bided his time for his own moment. Now she offered everything he'd been promised.

As though waiting for the lover's kiss, he sniffed the briny air. "Oh...she is that, my friend," he murmured. "More demanding than any other paramour. A courtesan who demands your very essence, who takes nothing less than everything."

"Well that she left the cargo intact, then. For my luck, you made it." Wiebe began moving back toward the slackening activity. "You'll push down the coast from here," he remarked, already knowing the answer as he handed Garrett a large satchel of correspondence and payment.

With a tilt to his head, Wiebe jiggled his three chins toward the leather bag. "There be a letter from the old captain himself in there for you."

A warning tingle traveled the length of Garrett spine. Retaining his cordial mask, he nodded. "We'll leave afore the tide completes."

They moved to the first of the line of three wagons, inspecting the contents. The barrels of French brandy would triple Wiebe's investment in a time when quality spirits were scarce. Political unrest created profitable business.

Inspection done and Wiebe appeased, Garrett returned to the cliff to scout the lightening horizon. From there he watched his old friend leave, safeguarding his future income.

Garrett returned his attention to the sea. From his vantage, she appeared as an innocuous mirror wherever his sight scanned. Only those familiar with her workings knew the deep disquiet under the surface. The sheltered cove hid their very existence, but that granted no guarantee of safety. The stakes seemed to escalate with each trip, and the business proved to be a certain tightrope he walked with a steady gait as he played each side against the other to achieve his end. His father entrusted him with their enterprise, and he refused to form allegiances with either faction.

With the breaking dawn turning the purple night to a rosy morning, he was ever more cautious as his keen eyes pierced the gloom. This was the most dangerous time of the day. From this vantage point, he could see far out to sea. Nothing. He relaxed his stance and filled his lungs with the fresh morning air peppered with the scents of the evergreen forest to his back and prepared to read the correspondence from his father.

"Capt'in." The huffed, slightly high-pitched voice

pulled him from his thoughts. Small pebbles cascaded down the steep slope, heralding the arrival of the young deck lad, no more than ten or twelve. "Capt'in McGuire, sir, as you see, the last of the wagons has left. Quartermaster's asking permission to grant the men their tot of rum."

Garrett spared the boy a brief glance. The lad appeared positively frightened standing before him with the light of the morning bouncing off the sweat sheen of his skin, brown eyes large in his face. Garrett hadn't been much older than this lad when his father shipped him off to sea to learn to be a man. "Tell Tippen I'll be down shortly. The men may have their tots by shifts, as I want sentries on board as well as on land until we sail."

"Aye, Capt'in."

His eyes returned to the boy, where he nodded once in dismissal.

The boy smiled, nodded his head, and stumbled back down the hill, seeming grateful to be away.

Garrett settled on a boulder, face to the breeze, and skimmed the correspondence in turn. His fingers paused at his father's letter. His sire's crisp penmanship graced the front of the parchment. Garrett turned the heavy envelope over, where his fingers played across the waxed family crest. Had he ever forgiven his father for giving up the sea when his mother died?

"If I can't have both," his father had said before he set Garrett upon his first ship under the watchful care and guidance of his father's man Burke, "then I'll have neither."

Garrett watched the lad slither down the face of the hill on his backside. Alone once more, he savored the weight of the document in brief contemplation of what news it might hold before breaking the distinctive family seal of the three ships, masts filled with wind, sailing to some unknown destination.

With a last glance to the horizon, he turned his gaze to his own three-masted, twelve-gunned brig-sloop. The *Isle Sky* was a strong, fast ship even when loaded down with the best liqueurs he could procure. He heard the general laughter and good-natured banter rise up on the breeze as news spread that the captain gave leave to enjoy a tot. With all that they had gone through on board these last weeks, his men deserved this slight reprieve.

The pending day's brightness raced like a chariot across the pink-hued sky, finally providing Garrett with enough light to read by. Relaxing his seat, he let his elbows rest upon his thighs as he set aside his mental list of what needed to be done before they set sail, to focus his attention on the letter in hand.

London, 17 March, 1798
Dear Son,
It is with a heavy heart that I must relay the most sad and painful intelligence. Your stepmother has died. She had become afflicted with the morbid sore throat shortly after the strong north winds brought the worst of the winter weather inland. Though a doctor was procured most immediately and she confined to her bed, she succumbed to her fever by the day's break just a fortnight ago.

Garrett rubbed at an imagined kink at the base of his neck, turning his scrutiny to the umbrella sky. He watched as dusty purple clouds skidded across the horizon, pondering the philosophical debate of heaven and hell. Which would the Lady Matilda forcefully enter? Her nasal whine was certain to draw attention from both directions. How very different she'd been from the fiery-haired beauty of his mother.

His father had married too soon in an effort to provide a mother to his young son and, once trapped, found every other occupation to give him solace.

Try as he might, Garrett could muster no great feeling of loss for the woman who had claimed the role of mother these last years. Without doubt, she had proven as much a disappointment in the role to him as she had been to his father in her inability to conceive a back-up heir.

In these last ten years that you have been away, you have provided evidence of a man capable of not only building a successful enterprise from our fleet, despite my misgivings of your methods, but expanding our merchant connections.

His father, now a well-respected Tory in the House, couldn't, given his own history, protest Garrett's seeming lack of loyalty to the Crown, evidenced further as he never refused the accumulated bounty that filled the family's coffers.

Though I know the pull of the sea, it is now past the time where you must return to your rightful place as my heir...

Despite his years, old Captain Mackenzie McGuire remained ever competitive to further the family fortunes, if not necessarily to wealth, certainly to the prestige of name. Garrett drew breath and wished he too had a tot of rum to quell the tightening of his gut. Here was the letter he had been dreading.

Garrett's hand fisted the corner of the missive, rolling and unrolling the edge as he controlled the sudden urge to set it aflame and pretend he'd never received the correspondence. Marry. As sole heir, his father expected him to return home to wed, produce legitimate sons, and continue the legacy. The matrimonial contract to Beverly MacLeod had been drawn up before his own mother's death birthing a brother who lived only long enough to draw a few short breaths. This legal pact would finally fulfill a longstanding family alliance to bridge the McGuire name to one of well-known heritage and provide a title to accompany and legitimize the wealth.

With their lands bordering one another's, he and the two MacLeod daughters, along with their older brother Brian, Garrett's lifelong friend, had been tossed together as children, growing up like a school of fish. Garrett being of an age with Brian, they'd both taken to the sea the same year, though on different vessels.

Garrett shook his head, struggling to continue through the lengthy missive. Despite his best efforts, which in fact represented little to no enthusiasm, he had no great regard for Beverly. True too, he remained in no doubt of her mutual disregard for him.

He rubbed the roughened stubble on his chin and tried to imagine his betrothed. *Bollocks.* Though it had been nigh on five years since he had last laid eyes upon her, he could not imagine she was anything more than the spoiled child she had been when he had last known her. Try as he might, thoughts of Beverly always brought to mind her younger sister Anne.

They too had lost a mother to childbirth. While they had seemed to be left to fend for themselves,

Beverly assumed the matron's role, while Anne ran wild, trying to convince himself and Brian she was equal to a boy and should be allowed to join their games.

Bessy the Brave, she had coined herself, as she strove to keep pace with him and her brother. Garrett traced a thumb along his lip, pinching back the smile as he recalled her scrappy use of her middle name as an identifier. He closed his eyes and easily remembered a face often soiled, skirts drawn up and tied to allow her the freedom to run until her nanny—or worse still, her sister—would find her out and report back to the household.

Roaming his fingers over the raised ink on the paper, he allowed the small smile to curve his lips. Anne never ran in fright from the scolding, but at the first opportunity, while he and Brian practiced swords or the like, her slight frame would be seen to slip away to the woods surrounding their property.

Sometimes he would follow. He couldn't help himself, curious, drawn to her nature, like one to a wood nymph. There he discovered the young girl, safely away from confines imposed in a rigid house, would come alive with exploration and wonder. How she had intrigued him when he was a young lad.

But he wasn't a young lad any longer. He was a grown man of four-and-twenty, and he'd been summoned home. At that moment Garrett felt the cuffs of society secure around his wrists. The jailer's whip at his back. There was no running away from his duty. Straightening his spine to the inevitable, he stood, preparing to return to the beach. He cast one last look to the horizon, and froze.

A word about the author…

Let's face it…Lori likes tea. Most often found in the kitchen sharing stories or in a coffee shop, mug in hand, she can visit for hours.

That's inspiration: people, places, adventure. Every day is made up of the moments to create the tapestry of life.

Without sharing, how would you ever know that Gord from a small farming community in Northern Alberta found himself in Australia on a tour and passed his childhood friend Joe hitchhiking? They pulled over, unbelieving that this could really be Joe, and sure enough: Joe on the side of the road, on the other side of the world, decades after they had last met. Great stories!

To be able to put thoughts on paper and have other people appreciate the stories, laugh, cry, feel the passion, is a dream come true for Lori Power.

Lori's body of work is as varied as the adventures of daily life and includes children's stories, a gluten-free cookbook, romance, suspense, and thrillers and soon to be Young Adult fiction.

Her first "official" novel, *Storms of Passion*, published by The Wild Rose Press under their Champagne line, was released in 2014.

Book One in the "Under Suspicion" series, beginning with *Hit 'n' Run*, followed by *The Tables Have Turned* is available now, from Limitless Publishing. Book Three, *Secrets Revealed*, is presently in process, and the series will be concluded with Book Four, *Finding Home*.

"The Gentle Surf" series is available from Wild

Ross Press. This includes *Sea Breeze*, inspired by the Hotel Del Coronado on the Southern tip of the California coast. *From the Front Desk*, Book Two, and the third installment in this series, *For a Song*, just released.

Collaboration is important to improving one's craft, and Lori is an active member of the TransCanada Romance Writers, Romance Writers of America, the Calgary chapter of the Romance Writers, and the Alberta Romance Writers Association and belongs to both a critiquing group and a beta reading weekly group.

In all things, remember...life is a journey. Thanks for being part of the adventure!

Thank you for purchasing
this publication of The Wild Rose Press, Inc.

For questions or more information
contact us at
info@thewildrosepress.com.

The Wild Rose Press, Inc.
www.thewildrosepress.com